THE PENALTY AREA

Alain Gillot

THE PENALTY AREA

*Translated from the French
by Howard Curtis*

Europa
editions

Europa Editions
214 West 29th Street
New York, N.Y. 10001
www.europaeditions.com
info@europaeditions.com

Copyright © 2015 by Flammarion, Paris
First Publication 2016 by Europa Editions

Translation by Howard Curtis
Original title: *La surface de réparation*
Translation copyright © 2016 by Europa Editions

Library of Congress Cataloging in Publication Data is available
ISBN 978-1-60945-353-4

Gillot, Alain
The Penalty Area

Book design by Emanuele Ragnisco
www.mekkanografici.com

Cover illustration by Mariachiara Di Giorgio

Prepress by Grafica Punto Print – Rome

Printed in the USA

"They want you dead, or in their lie.
There's only one thing a man can do.
Find something that's his,
and make an island for himself."
—Sergeant Welsh in Terrence Malick's film *The Red Line*

To Caroline, and the family she believed in

THE PENALTY AREA

1

Hamed came straight up to me, striding like a frustrated young horse. It was almost the end of the summer vacation, and for a week now it had been raining cats and dogs. The kids were already finding it hard enough to concentrate. If on top of that they had to play in a quagmire, that would be the end of it.

"No way to get a foothold, sir. Any pass you try, you end up on your ass."

The players always need to talk. About a scratch, about the kit, the conditions. Some days, they just want to go back to the locker room.

"Show me your cleats."

He turned his back to me and lifted one leg, and I glanced at the sole of his boot.

"They look small to me."

"They're the ones I always have, sir."

"And you haven't noticed anything since Monday?"

"Well . . . it hasn't stopped raining."

"And what do you think you should have done?"

"Put on bigger ones."

"So now go back and do your best to stay on your feet."

His eyes went up in their sockets. Hamed has that stubborn streak that leads him to drive straight into the defense instead of lifting his head and looking for an unmarked teammate. I have twenty-three like him to deal with, and there are days when I wonder what I'm doing here, looking after a gang of brats who'll never become real soccer players.

It's my second experience as a coach since I obtained my federal diploma. The first time was in Limoges with the top-division amateur team. Postmen who worked all week and came for training in the evenings. But I got tired of that schedule. So when I came across an ad in *France Football*, "Sedan Club seeks qualified instructor to handle its youth team, aged from ten to fourteen." I thought it might be right for me. Not that I'm especially fond of kids. I don't have any myself, and can take or leave them, but the salary was decent, and the fact that a house was included in the conditions clinched the deal for me.

Obviously, Sedan has its limitations. The club is long past its glory days and they won't be coming back anytime soon. The premier team is in the second division, close to the bottom of the table. They need to find a little nugget. A player who'd give the supporters something to hope for, and drag the other team members up to a higher level. That's what happened in Nancy with Platini. But a Platini comes along once every fifty years, and he's unlikely to show up in Sedan. What I'm dealing with is kids like Kevin Rouverand. He's the striker of the group—on a good day, at least. Less than five feet tall, a very low center of gravity, a killer right foot. He could really amount to something, but, as far as motivation goes, forget it. He strolls onto the field with that small talent of his, as if he has all the time in the world. Like a lot of his friends, he's waiting for an offer from an important club. He skims through auto magazines, taps away on his cell phone, sculpts his hair with gel. He thinks he's already arrived, when he hasn't even gotten on the train.

I thought the rain was finally going to stop, but in fact it got even heavier, so I blew the whistle and collected the bibs. I didn't want them to catch cold. The group was already decimated enough.

"See you tomorrow," Kevin cried.

"See you tomorrow, try not to be late."

He was already engrossed in his text messages. At first, that kind of behavior drove me crazy, but now I've developed a bit of perspective. It's a generational thing. There are no more sons of miners. That doesn't mean that young guys today have no aims, they want to make money, soon they'll want girls. But that's just an incentive, and to have a career you need more than that.

My own career stopped dead one Sunday in April, nearly ten years ago, when I was playing for Limeil-Brévannes. I'd just turned twenty-nine and the management of Martigues had already made an offer for me. A whole season's trial, with an option on the following season, and I was feeling fairly confident about the future, until the other team's center back destroyed that promised transfer by pressing down with all his weight on my left knee.

The guy's name was Didier M'bati. He was originally from Ghana and must have weighed at least two hundred pounds. As I lay writhing in pain, he kept repeating that he hadn't done it deliberately, and it was true. I'd tried to wrong-foot him, but my leg was in an awkward position and he'd stepped on it, just because he'd built up speed and couldn't stop. I was operated on in Dijon, where recovery times were known to be quicker, but in my case they soon realized it was going to take more than a week. The damage was too extensive and, after various tests, the doctors confirmed that I'd never play soccer again. I'd be able to walk well enough, but from now on running would be a risky venture.

That opened the door to depression. I went into a spiral where I'd sleep almost all day and come to life only at night. I took the phone off the hook. I stopped washing myself, ate out of cans. Gradually, I got out of my depth and ended up taking refuge in drink, even though I'd always hated being drunk before. I started hanging out in bars, until the day I got into a

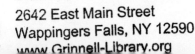

fight with a guy, without even knowing why. They had to hold me back, I didn't even see how badly I'd messed him up. I ended up in the police station, in a holding cell. Things would have gotten worse if something hadn't happened that night. Lying on that straw mattress that smelled of piss, I had a weird dream. I was alone in the middle of a silent stadium, tracing white lines with a machine that squeaked with each turn of the wheel. I was taking my time, applying myself. Then, when my work was over, I sat down in the middle of the field and stayed there, feeling a sense of peace I'd never known before. As if the white lines were ramparts that protected me from everything.

When I woke up, I remembered the dream. It was like a revelation. Being a player wasn't the most important thing. What I missed wasn't the game itself, it was no longer being in that space where I felt safe. I just had to get back on the field and everything would be okay. And at noon, when the cops released me, my one thought was to call the Federation and inquire how to go about obtaining a qualification as a coach.

"Is it okay if I lock up the locker room, Monsieur Barteau?"

It was the keeper of the stadium. He was just behind me, in the fading light.

"Go ahead, Émile."

"Did you get your car back in the end?"

"No, but Meunier's going to drive me home. Have a good evening."

I stayed there for another little while until the lights went out. The rain was still falling steadily, and a pool was starting to form in the penalty area. Things weren't looking good for tomorrow.

2

I crossed the deserted parking lot and walked to the bus stop, or what was left of it. Ever since the town council had decided to do away with the route, the stop had been badly vandalized. The glass walls were shattered and the bench burned, but the roof was still there, and I wedged myself under it to shelter from the rain. Even though it wasn't very late, the cement works had already closed its doors, and, as that was the one activity in the area, there was total silence on the plateau. It reminded me of the times I used to run away as a boy, venturing as far as possible from home and hiding out in a park or under a bridge, listening and watching. As it happens, it was thanks to one of these escapades that I'd discovered soccer. That time, my father had surpassed himself. No sooner had he sat down at the table than he flung away the plates and everything on them because the mayonnaise was the wrong brand. I never missed an opportunity, so I looked him straight in the eyes, and of course he couldn't stand that. He started running after me, taking off his belt and banging it on the walls, a real performance. And since I already knew how my mother was going to react—look away, launch into a thorough clean-up of the kitchen, everything, in fact, except intervene—I went out through the garden gate, walked along the railroad tracks, then crossed the highway and ventured into the Grassin neighborhood, which I'd never dared explore before.

When my parents talked about the place, it was always to say something bad about it. According to them, it was the lair of drug dealers and car thieves, and I'd even heard them say that a girl had been found in a garbage can there with her throat cut. But that day, driven by rage, I walked like an automaton along abandoned streets, and down an avenue that seemed endless, where the houses had closed shutters or boarded-up windows. I came to a kind of traffic circle, occupied by a car without wheels. I really was a long way from home, and it was almost dark. I was unsure whether or not to continue, but then something caught my attention, a big pole with floodlights on it. I advanced to the end of the plateau, and there, down below, I saw the sports fields. There were three of them, immaculately laid out.

I hurtled down the slope through the wild grasses, and moved closer to a handful of guys, no more than four or five of them, practicing corner kicks. They must have been about twenty, and they all wore shirts from one or other of the clubs they worshiped. Manchester United, Barcelona, AC Milan. They yelled jokes at each other as they kicked the ball. It wasn't an intensive training session. Sometimes they sped up the game to land a shot, a one-two, sometimes they stopped and chatted, and at the end they lay down on the grass for a series of stretching exercises and one of them told a story that provoked gales of laughter. They hadn't spotted me, or else they didn't care about my presence. I stayed there until night fell, watching them from a distance. I saw them start playing again, stringing together volleys and some more or less successful lobs, and strutting like victors after a between-the-legs pass or a back heel. As I made my way home, I was so obsessed by what I'd just experienced that I didn't feel the cold, even though it was November, or any kind of fear as I walked back through those deserted neighborhoods. I went in through the gate and found my mother in her kitchen, brushing the tiles so hard she could easily have broken a nail, and my father sprawled on the couch, open-mouthed, staring drunkenly at his stupid TV show, harmless for now—not that it mattered anymore, because I was out of reach. I'd found a world of my own.

A pencil of light cut through the darkness, and two head-lights appeared at the end of the line. It was Meunier. I was almost surprised that he was there so soon. He pulled up level with me, and as he leaned across to open the door he gave me much too broad a smile, so broad I wondered who it was meant for.

I realized as soon as I sat down. The car smelled so new, it was nauseating. He needed to show me his new toy. It couldn't wait. That was why he'd offered to drive me home.

"Give me your address," he said.

"Don't you remember where I live?"

"Yes, but I want you to see something, the latest sat nav. It shows you your route in 3D, it's amazing."

I looked at him to see if he was serious. Of course he was.

"Guess how much I paid for it? You won't believe it."

"Ten thousand."

"Are you crazy, ten thousand won't get you anything these days!"

"I paid six for mine."

"Yours is a wreck. And it's always leaving you high and dry. I got this one for twenty-two thousand even though it's worth seven more. With this crisis, people are ready to do anything to make money. So, are you going to give me that address?"

Meunier had lived at my place for three months. He'd been hired as an accountant by the club and, as none of the available accommodation was right for him, the management had asked me if I was prepared to put him up until they found him some-where suitable. Ever since, he'd been acting as if we were friends, even though the one thing those months had demon-strated to me was how different we were. He was the kind of person who'd go out in the evening and come back late, whereas I preferred to stay home. He never refilled the refrigerator, and spent most of his time walking up and down, phone glued to his ear, talking about personal things as if I wasn't there. By the time he handed back his keys, I was relieved.

"Now don't be stupid, you're coming with me tonight!"

"Don't count on me. I've been getting wet all day."

"Quit fooling, wait 'til you see the girls!"

"Good for you."

"Stop it, don't tell me you don't care. How long is it since you last got laid? We're both men, we can tell each other these things, can't we? So how long is it? Six months? A year?"

As he talked, I saw a medallion swinging from the rear-view mirror. It was a group photograph of his wife and kids inside a pink plastic heart.

"Your sat nav isn't working," I said, watching the car advance in 3D on the little high-definition screen. "We're several miles out."

"Impossible."

"It's twice as quick if you go via the station."

"Have you ever been married?"

"No."

"It's funny, we shared a house and I don't know anything about your life. You have lived with a woman at some point, haven't you?"

"Yes."

"And?"

"It's not my thing."

I suddenly realized he hadn't only bought a car. He'd also bought a suit whose color matched the upholstery, an impressive pearl gray. At the lights, he gazed at himself in the rear-view mirror, chin lifted triumphantly.

"Are you a fag? No, I'm joking . . . Come on, make a bit of an effort. You know the new girl in accounting has the hots for you?"

"Great."

"Don't you care?"

"Not especially."

"Do you think badly of me?"

"For what?"

"Cheating on my wife."

"That's your problem."

"It's my problem, but you wouldn't do it."

"I have no way of knowing, I don't live with anyone. You can drop me here. It's one-way from here on."

He pulled up at the corner of the street. He wanted to talk some more, but I didn't give him the chance. I quickly got out of the car.

3

On foot, there was less than two hundred yards to go before I got to Rue des Platanes, where my house was. I was going to take a very hot bath, to get rid of all that cold and rain, make myself a TV dinner, and watch a good movie, preferably a comedy, or maybe go straight to bed. What could stop me? Nothing.

I knew the blonde in accounting was stuck on me. I'd seen her several times in the club's offices, and she always arranged it so that she was around when I was waiting to see the chairman. But I wasn't interested. I wasn't a monk, I wasn't insensitive to female charms. But since I'd moved to Sedan, I'd decided that if I was a loner, I should live up to it. Once and for all. That hadn't always been the case, in spite of what Meunier might have thought. I'd had a fair number of flings, I'd even lived with someone, but nothing had worked out. Why did I find it so hard to connect with another person? It was a question I'd often asked myself. Was it because of my family history? Or just my character? Probably a bit of both.

Even back in the days when I'd first trained, I'd go for a drink with the guys in my class and watch them from a distance as they went about picking up girls. They were pretty good at it, but I preferred to stay perched on my stool. I was too touchy, too jealous of my own independence to get involved with anyone. With time, though, I did go down into the arena. When you're a soccer player, there are always girls hanging around you, and it's easier to say yes than no. I'd had affairs with all kinds of girls, nice ones, bad-tempered ones, weird ones, without becoming attached to any of them. In the end, this reluctance started to feel like a burden, and I decided to live with someone, as a challenge.

Her name was Sophie Pinton and she was the daughter of the chairman of the Limoges club, who was sympathetic to the idea of my settling down. Sophie was very kind and funny, at least at the start of our relationship. She was the ideal person to try my luck with, and I made a real effort for it to work. I bought myself shirts. I repainted the walls of an apartment, put up shelves, chose a couch to match the curtains, agreed to discuss vacation destinations, repaired plugs, went to dinner at her parents' house on Sunday evenings. All those things that help you to be accepted in society, to be considered a well-balanced person. I played the game as long as possible. And then one day, Sophie asked me if I'd give her a child and I realized my limits. In the middle of the night, I had an anxiety attack I couldn't control. It was stifling, even with the window wide open, and my unease just kept getting worse, I had no other choice but to walk out and take refuge in a hotel, where I gradually recovered and my newly regained solitude, far from weighing on me, seemed like a liberation. Hadn't I always been alone? Way back in my own family. In the schoolyard, too. So I might as well accept my condition, rather than make futile efforts to pretend. And as far as my relations with women were concerned, I had to admit in the end that, apart from the sex, the most I was capable of was a kind of friendship. But the door always had to remain open, and, when she wanted more, all I could do was pack my bags and try to hurt her as little as possible.

Once, just once, I'd felt something that might have resembled love. It was soon after I'd moved to Créteil to play in the national championships. Thanks to the club, I'd just moved into a two-room apartment in a development close to the municipal stadium. I moved in almost at the same time as an art history student from Croatia, who'd come to France to get her diploma. I helped her carry her boxes up the stairs. Her name was Mila Brekjovic and her face was partially disfigured. She told me later that it had happened during the war, but wouldn't say any more than that. As far as I was concerned, she was really beautiful. She had the most amazing eyes. Our relationship gradually developed through a series of everyday events. First, we ran into each other in the laundromat, then, one day, her mail was put in my box by mistake and I rang her doorbell to hand it over to her. We started exchanging smiles when we met by chance, plus a few banal words to be polite. Although we never went beyond that, I felt strangely close to her. Was it because she was a foreigner? All those people who were settled, sure of their place, scared me. There was something reassuring about the way Mila just seemed to be passing through, her whole world contained in a suitcase. Plus, she'd been through a war, she knew what things could be hidden behind immaculate house fronts and neat gardens. One evening, an electricity blackout hit the whole block, and she must have felt emboldened. We shared a candle in my kitchen and, by way of a meal, a simple can of sardines. But then I let her go home. What stopped me from taking her in my arms? What was I waiting for? I finally persuaded myself that I had to at least try. I made up my mind to ask her out on a date when I got back from a tournament in the south where the club had a fixture. But when I did get back, there was a note under my door. She'd returned to her country. She thanked me for everything. I stood there, rooted to the spot, holding that note and reading it over and over. It really hurt. It was as if I'd lost the one person I trusted, the one person I could have had a connection with.

All at once, shouts jolted me back to the present, to Rue des Platanes, and I peered into the darkness to see where they were coming from. From a house opposite. The living room window was open and you could see a woman standing under the overhead light, her head bowed, and a man walking back and forth in front of her and waving his arms. They were obviously quarreling. Then the man realized their privacy was on display and closed the window. I smiled in spite of myself. That was exactly what my father always did before he exploded: check that the door and windows were closed, so that there was no chance our little personal hell would arouse our neighbors' curiosity. I opened the gate and strode across the garden.

Once in the house, I switched on the light in the corridor and went straight to the bathroom. I turned the faucets in the bath full on, and had started taking off my jacket and my shoes when the front door bell rang. Who could it possibly be? I wasn't expecting anyone, especially not at that hour. It had to be a mistake. My neighbor had taken the number off his gate, and people easily got it wrong.

I opened the door. A woman was standing there. It took me a moment or two to recognize her, because the garden was dark. Plus, her hair was a different color. It wasn't a mistake, at least not a mistake with the number. It was my sister Madeleine.

4

I remembered her being the nervous kind, but never quite like this. Madeleine went straight to the living room, made as if to sit down, then changed her mind, as if the couch was burning hot. She dove into her bag and started talking, with her nose in her things.

"Do you have a cigarette?"

"I'd already quit smoking the last time we met, and that must have been at least two years ago."

"As long as that?"

"Yes."

"We've talked on the phone, though."

"Argued, you mean. How did you get here?"

"Someone lent me a car."

She was blonde now. But she'd kept her chestnut-brown eyebrows. It was obvious that something was wrong. "Are you still in Saint-Quentin with your mother?"

"No, I'm back in Paris. Why don't you say 'Ma'?"

"It doesn't feel natural."

She finally sat down. I remained standing. Nothing had ever been easy between us. Madeleine was my older sister, by five years, and it had always felt to me as if we hadn't been brought up under the same roof. In those early years, there was too much of an age difference for us to really share anything, and by the time we moved to Saint-Quentin she was already a teenager, and my mother had urged her to go to a vocational college to learn secretarial work. She was a boarder there and

I only saw her on weekends, if you could use the word "see":
She'd shut herself up in her room and only come out of it to go
straight into the bathroom and "get ready," as she put it. At
mealtimes, she never ate anything, just sat looking out the window, as if Prince Charming was going to appear at any
moment. My father would make comments about the length of
her skirts, but she always managed to avoid confrontation. She
was clever at that, much more than I was. She'd come and go
and never let herself be trapped. And then once she got her
diploma, she moved to Paris to do office work. All of which
meant that she'd known nothing, or very little, about the
nuclear war that had broken out in our house soon after we
moved to Saint-Quentin. It's quite simple: As far as she was
concerned, our parents were frozen in time, like figurines on a
mantelpiece. She hadn't noticed that my father's suits had
started to look threadbare, that he hid bottles in the closets, or
that my mother was living on pills.

"You absolutely have to help me out. I'm in deep shit."

"Do you need money?"

"No, it's not that. I've managed to get onto a course. Ten
days of total immersion. I'll have a real chance of finding work
again. But it's the school vacation, and I have my kid. A girlfriend of mine was supposed to take him in, but she let me
down at the last moment."

"Have someone watch him."

"It's obvious you don't have a kid. You know how much a
full-time babysitter costs? And you try finding one at short
notice."

"Is it that urgent?"

"I start my course the day after tomorrow."

"Why don't you take him to Saint-Quentin?"

"Ma's back in the hospital."

"Weren't you with a guy? Weren't you supposed to be
going to South America together?"

"We broke up."

Silence fell over the room. Madeleine had found her cigarettes. I saw that her hand was shaking a little, that she was breathing in the smoke and blowing it out too hard. She'd put on foundation to give herself some color, but had applied it unevenly. It stopped at the jawline, and the top of her neck was white. It was as if she was wearing a mask. I was summing things up in my mind. She was out of work. Her guy had dumped her. How old was her son? And what on earth was his name?

"Léonard. He's thirteen."

"What?"

"You're trying to remember my son's name and age. His name's Léonard and he's thirteen."

"Hold on . . . Where is he now?"

"In the car."

"You're joking."

She'd always had a nerve. As a child, I'd seen her stealing from my mother's purse and then shamelessly asking her for pocket money not long afterwards.

"Go get him right now."

"So you will take him?"

"I didn't say that!"

"If you haven't made up your mind, it's best he doesn't come in."

"You left your kid in a car."

"He loves it."

"What?"

"He loves being alone in an enclosed space. It's what he prefers. But he hates situations that aren't clear. If he sees you hesitate, he'll freak out."

I felt anger rising inside me, but managed to control it. "I have to turn off my bath."

"I'm sorry, Vincent. If there was any other way—"

"I haven't said yes."

I went back to the bathroom and turned off the faucets. I sat down on the edge of the bath. Ten days wasn't the end of the world, but it was her behavior that upset me, that way she had of coming back into my life without warning. When I went back out to the living room, Madeleine was still in the same position on the edge of the couch. She was like a puppet whose strings had been cut.

"I have a suggestion. You can sleep here. You aren't going to drive tonight anyway, and that way we'll have time to talk."

"Talk about what?"

"Your son. Your situation."

"You don't trust—"

"No."

Madeleine realized she had no choice. She nodded and stood up. She walked straight to the door. It wasn't what she'd imagined. She'd thought she could just waltz in and take me by surprise, dump her son on me, and walk off again, before I'd taken it all in. Instead of which, she was going to have to stay a while. With a brother who wasn't going to make things easy for her.

5

I went to the doorway to see what my nephew looked like. I realized why I hadn't seen Madeleine when I got home. She'd parked on the other side of the street, a little farther down. The car she'd been lent was an ancient Renault 18. I had no idea they were still in circulation.

Madeleine opened the door on the passenger side and her son got out. She said something to him, clearly to inform him of the arrangement, then took a big bag from the trunk. They walked toward me. I felt as if I was in some kind of science-fiction movie. I'd be waking up any moment.

"Léonard, this is my brother Vincent."

"Hello, Léonard."

I couldn't catch his eyes. I wondered if he was shy, or upset by the situation. Surely both.

"He's always on the moon," my sister said. "People often think he's rude. But he isn't, he's just miles away."

"I didn't say anything."

I let them go ahead of me into the house. Léonard had an oddly shaped head. It was as if he had an adult's cranium stuck on a child's neck. Now all three of us were in the living room.

"Would you like something to eat?"

"We ate all kinds of junk on the way. And besides, Léonard is used to going to bed very early. He generally sleeps a lot."

It was now Léonard's whole face I found intriguing. It was completely devoid of emotion.

"Then let me show him his room."

I went ahead down the corridor that led to the bedrooms in back; there were three of them, including one that was quite big, the one Meunier had occupied. It was because of a misunderstanding that I had such a large house. The management of the club had mixed up my application with another candidate's, a father of three, and the local council had offered me a four-bedroom house as a result. Of course, by the time I arrived in Sedan, the club had realized its mistake, but there wasn't a lot of accommodation available, which meant that I'd kept the house, with the possibility that I'd move in the end. But I hadn't heard any more about it, and so I'd stayed.

I turned to face my sister. She'd done her best to appear in top shape when she rang my bell, but now she looked completely exhausted.

"He can have one of the two small bedrooms. Whichever he prefers. You can take the large one."

"Don't give him a choice. He doesn't like that."

My sister went into the nearest bedroom. She put the big bag down in the middle of the room and started rummaging through it. The boy sat down on the edge of the bed.

Léonard was like a cosmonaut. The image occurred to me because of the way he held himself. He was wearing only a slicker over a woolen sweater, but it was as if his clothes weighed tons and his movements were limited. What did his voice sound like? I still hadn't heard it. His eyes had stopped roving and had come to rest on a specific point. His mother's hand, busy sorting through his things and hers. He was waiting for something. He started moving his right leg up and down, faster and faster, then suddenly stopped when Madeleine handed him a small box covered in black imitation leather.

"I'll get the sheets," I said.

"He can sleep like that, you know."

"I have a whole stock of them I never do anything with. Might as well use them."

When I moved into the house, I'd observed that it was already furnished and that everything I'd need in daily life had been provided, from vacuum cleaner to forks, by way of bedding, and there was practically nothing to buy. Which was fine by me. I'd never bothered to make a place mine, surrounding myself with personal objects.

I opened the big closet in the laundry room. There was enough to make beds for a whole regiment. Everything was folded and spotlessly clean.

Léonard was already asleep by the time I went back into the bedroom. He was lying curled up, wrapped in the quilt, the black box next to him.

"When he's sleepy, he just drops off."

It was my sister's voice from the bathroom, where she was putting out her son's toiletries.

"You won't have to tidy up after him. He's very clean. He doesn't like people touching his things anyway. He can throw a fit over a toothbrush that's askew."

"Don't act as if I've agreed."

"Sorry."

She turned her back to me, and her gestures slowed down. I sensed she was taking in what I'd just said.

I glanced at the bed, at this boy who'd somehow forced his way into my house. He was breathing hard. Beneath his closed eyelids, the nerves throbbed.

"Did you choose this wallpaper?"

"No. It was already here."

"Horrible, isn't it?"

"This is the first time anybody's slept in this room. I only come in here to air it."

"So you still live alone?"

"As you can see."

I looked at the room as if seeing it for the first time—which I was. An old woman must have lived in it. The furniture was from the fifties, and the china trinkets wouldn't have withstood a child. The wallpaper really was hideous, disturbing even. I wondered if a kid waking up here would be scared by those monstrous flowers. But I dismissed the thought. It was only for one night.

6

I had a look in the fridge to see what was left. I hadn't been shopping for several days, and it was starting to become obvious. All the same, I found some boiled potatoes, a little lettuce, a piece of cheese, and some eggs. I could make an omelet. Behind my back, I could feel my sister watching me.

"What is this training course exactly?"

"It's about computer tools. If you don't follow the latest changes in hardware, you have no chance. People are already fighting over the smallest jobs."

"I thought you had a great job in that mail-order company. Weren't you supposed to be getting a promotion?"

Hearing the chair squeak, I knew what she was doing. Whenever she started telling a story, she couldn't stop fidgeting, as if she was looking for a position she couldn't find.

"God, that place was hell! I even had to work weekends. I was going crazy. I was supposed to be made head of department. I didn't make that up! But one Monday morning, when we opened, the cops showed up. I called the boss on all his phones. Vanished into thin air. He'd been cheating for years, fake invoices, check kiting, the whole thing . . . "

Madeleine's stories all had something in common. They started out with lucrative prospects, then things got confused, and it all ended up down the drain.

"And that was when you went back to Paris."

"Yes. A girlfriend suggested I share her job part-time. Her guy had just walked out so she could put me up, too.

She wanted to go into something else, but without giving up her job. Except it didn't work out and she went back to working full-time. I'm still living at her place. The Renault is her car."

"So now you don't have anything."

"I have unemployment benefits, but not for much longer. I can't mess up this course."

I threw the eggs over the potatoes and the omelet came together. I put the bread, cheese, and lettuce on the table. I sat down opposite my sister and started eating.

"Are you sure you don't want anything?"

"Now that I see you, I'm hungry."

"Then grab a plate."

I divided my omelet in half and slid part of it onto her plate.

"I wouldn't like to deprive you of it."

"You should have told me that before."

"You see—"

"Eat."

Madeleine threw herself on the food. There she was, in flesh and blood, in my kitchen. I had to stay wide awake and think ahead about the possible effects of this intrusion. Whenever my sister had come back into my life, there had been consequences. Usually disastrous ones.

"You make them like Ma. A little runny."

"What are you talking about?"

"She used to make omelets just like—"

"That's enough, let's talk about something else, all right?"

She made an effort to chew without opening her mouth.

There was no more sound in the house. There we were, the two of us, facing each other across the round table. The garbage truck passed on the street. That was all you could hear.

"She's sick, you know. Her cancer's come back. Chemotherapy and everything."

"If you talk about her further, I'll throw you out."

Madeleine stopped her fork in mid-air. She'd thought I'd give her a bit more leeway, but she'd been wrong.

"You have to understand one thing. You'll never be able to make me feel sorry for her. And her illness doesn't change a thing. She brought her cancer on herself. It's what she did that's eating away at her, or rather what she didn't do."

"You can't say that."

"Yes, I can. I'm not asking you to think like me. I haven't come looking for you. You've lived your life, and I've lived mine. That's all. We have nothing to say to each other, nothing to share, not on that side anyway. Haven't you understood that in all this time?"

"No. I must be stupid."

Her mouth started quivering. All at once she was a little girl again. That was all I needed.

"What's the other side?"

"Huh?"

"The side we *can* share."

"If you stop always making the past sound better than it was, there may be one."

I saw she was tempted to answer me, but then had second thoughts. She really didn't have the strength. She ate a last mouthful, more slowly, grimacing as if she found it hard to swallow. I noticed something unusual. She'd always been well-groomed, but now her nails were dirty. She must have had to tinker with the Renault to get all the way here.

"You should have some cheese."

"No, I'm fine. I'm really grateful. I think I'll go to bed."

"If you aren't warm enough with one blanket, there are others in the closet. If you want to take a shower, you have to let the water run for a while until it gets hot."

She stood up. She hesitated about whether to come around the table and kiss me. She preferred not to take the risk. She must have thought I was going to bite.

"Good night, then. And thanks."

"For what?"

"Not leaving us outside."

"What do you take me for?"

7

I went straight to bed and switched out the light. I thought at first it was going to work, and then I realized I was wrong. My fists were clenched, as if I was at the dentist's, and my eyes were wide open. The past had come into the room.

I'd seen my mother for the last time on July 8, 1998, while the World Cup was still on: It was the day of the France-Croatia semi-final. By then, I was only going to Saint-Quentin once a year, and I always arranged it so that I showed up unexpectedly. I'd call, see if my father was there, and if he was out, I'd drop by. It was a matter of take it or leave it, and my mother knew that.

It happened to be her birthday. That was pure chance, I didn't realize it until the last moment, but it was too late to turn back, and in a way that's what set the whole thing off. Because, of course, she'd bought a cake to make my visit into a bit of a celebration, and so that was it, we celebrated.

At first, things went fairly well. My mother still had a way of making me feel sorry for her. You mustn't think it's always easy to be in a rage. Sometimes it's good to discover you can be as much of an idiot as anybody else. It's like gorging on sugar candies while watching some dumb comedy. You know perfectly well you're going to feel sick and you won't remember anything about the movie, but it makes you feel good at the time. That's the kind of thing I was looking for that day, knowing full well what I was playing at and happy to go along with it.

The weather was wonderful and we sat out in the garden. My mother had put on a flowered dress for the occasion, which made her look younger. She kept talking, but I wasn't listening. I was looking at her. I'd always been touched by how small she was. When she sat down on a chair, her legs didn't touch the ground, and when she was in a mischievous mood, which occasionally happened, she'd knock her calves together like a little girl. Obviously, I wasn't fooled. Little girls could be as calculating as adults, maybe even more so, and as far as that went, my mother was a queen, a queen in Saint-Quentin, in a house with unstable foundations, but a queen all the same. I knew it, and all the pitiful consequences that followed from it, but I needed to feel touched, and I'd decided to grant myself that pleasure, in that garden, that afternoon.

We even talked about my sister, her love affairs and mine, my work, all those things that people talk about without anything unpleasant rearing its head.

And then, just when I least expected it, maybe for the very reason that I'd lowered my guard, a single sentence turned everything upside down. Why did I suddenly pay attention at that moment? Why did I hear that sentence rather than any other? Because the sun had gone in? Because I didn't like the sparkling wine we were drinking? Because you can never get away from yourself for long?

My mother said, in that shrill voice of hers, "In spite of everything, we had some good times, didn't we?" That was how it started.

I said nothing for a moment or two, as if I had to let that sentence reach my brain. I looked at her for a long time to see if she'd noticed the effect her words had made. I saw her face turn white, as if sensing disaster.

I sighed, shook my head a little, like a boxer who realizes that the match won't be over until he's knocked out his opponent, and started to answer her, in a calm, almost detached voice.

Actually, it wasn't an answer so much as an indictment. Everything went into it, methodically, precisely, everything I blamed on my childhood. The humiliations, the prohibitions, the lack of understanding: I didn't leave anything out, from the little wounds to my self-esteem to the terrible day my father broke my arm by throwing me down the stairs, like a puppet, and I had to tell the surgeon, friends of the family, and even my school friends, that I'd slipped and fallen.

At first, my mother tried to protest, to present a more balanced point of view, to remind me of days by the sea, after-school snacks, handmade gifts, the times I'd been ill and caused them a lot of worry, anything she could think of that might serve as a counterblast, but little by little she gave up and withdrew into herself. The little girl gave way to an inadequate mother, and by the end of it there was nothing left on that chair but an old woman, her slice of cake in front of her, barely started, the candle melted on the chocolate, and we both realized that this birthday was actually a funeral. I'd buried our shared story and covered it in quicklime.

I left soon afterwards. She insisted on walking to the door, as if to share another few yards, another few seconds with her son, and when I was out on the sidewalk she said, "See you soon," in a muted voice, not even believing it herself.

On the train back to Paris, I sat for a long time as if in a daze. Did I really have all those things inside of me, after all these years? Maybe if that clarification had happened a little earlier in our lives, I would have considered it beneficial, but now all I felt was a rising sense of disgust. Reminding my mother just how much she had abandoned us, how hostile that house had been, couldn't bring me anything now but sadness. It was too late to make amends. It was too late to take revenge. The best thing I could do was make a clean break with my childhood, and that travesty of a family. The decision saved my life. Going back to that battlefield had been a big mistake, and I vowed, on the train, never to make it again.

I heard a slight noise. In other circumstances, it wouldn't have reached my ears, but memory had sharpened my senses. It was the sound of metal, coming from the kitchen. I got out of bed, put on a dressing down, opened my door, and walked to the kitchen down the dimly lit corridor. There was no trace of a presence, or any disturbance, but looking closer, I saw that the bread had been carefully cut and a piece was missing. I immediately thought of Léonard. He had gone to bed without eating. Maybe he'd felt the need to have a bite of something, but hadn't dared open the fridge.

I headed back to the bedrooms. Sure enough, the light was on in Léonard's room. A fleeting image came to me as I walked down the corridor. How many times, as a child, had I made night-time expeditions to the kitchen to grab a jar of jam, chocolate, cookies, whatever I could find, then run back to my room and eat that pirate feast under my bed by the light of a pocket torch, while planning my escape?

I came level with the door. Léonard was sitting on the bed, cross-legged, with his back to me. He had opened the black box that had intrigued me and laid it out in front of him. It was a chess set. He was completely engrossed. He was taking turns as both players, and checking each one's time with the help of a stopwatch. He wasn't aware of my presence and I could watch him for as long as I wanted. It was fascinating. He moved the pieces with striking precision and speed, never taking more than a few seconds to think.

I saw that the piece of bread was next to him. He'd munch some of it at regular intervals. He'd almost finished it. I retreated to the kitchen and put together a snack. A bit of salty and a bit of sweet, of course. A fizzy drink full of unmentionable chemicals, the kind that boys can't get enough of.

I went back to the bedroom, tray in hand, and stopped just

before the door. Léonard still hadn't noticed my presence and I wondered what I should do. Cough, say something to let him know I was there, walk into the room as naturally as possible? I was still trying to make up my mind when I heard his voice. He hadn't interrupted his game or changed his position.

"Can you play?"

His voice threw me. It was closer to that of an adult than a boy his age.

"No," I replied, advancing into the room.

I put the plate down on the bed, while he continued moving the pieces. The board was almost empty and it was all down to the bishop and a knight, assuming I'd identified them correctly. I didn't think he'd seen the tray because he was concentrating so hard on the game, but, without taking his eyes off the board, he grabbed a piece of cheese and wolfed it down.

"Are you afraid you won't understand?"

"I'm sorry?"

"Adults say they don't want to play, but it's a lie. They're afraid they won't understand. I can teach you, if you like."

I looked at his face for a trace of irony, or arrogance, but couldn't see anything like that. As I'd already observed when he arrived, he had a way of not showing his feelings, or maybe he just didn't have any. In fact he seemed to have already forgotten me after that brief sequence of verbal communication. He was again immersed in his world, concentrating on the game he was playing with and against himself.

I left the room and he didn't seem to notice. Yes, I'd have to do something about that wallpaper one day. It was two o'clock in the morning. The rain was coming down again. I heard it lashing the windowpanes. I got back into bed. In my job, I dealt with lots of kids, but none of them was anything like this one.

8

In the morning, the sky was bright blue. The wind had swept everything clean during the night. I walked around the deserted streets looking for a grocery that was open. I bought some cornflakes and orange juice, then made a detour via the bakery to get some brioches. I had everything I wanted.

By the time I got back home, my sister was already up, and was struggling with the coffee machine. Par for the course so far, but what aroused my curiosity was that she'd put on her raincoat and her big bag stood in the middle of the hall.

"What are you doing?"

"Making myself coffee. Trying, anyhow. I don't think this thing of yours is working."

"You have to hit it hard to get it started. You look like you're ready to leave."

"I have a long drive ahead of me. I'll drink my coffee and then wake Léonard at the last moment. He can finish sleeping in the car."

"You mean you're taking him with you?"

"I think it's for the best. I came here in a rush. You know me, I've always been impulsive. I was in a bit of a panic."

"And now you're not?"

"Yes, I am. But I realized it was a bad idea."

I put everything down on the table. What I wanted more than anything was to keep calm. "Can you tell me why?"

"Why it's a bad idea?"

"Yes."

She turned to me and gave a slight smile, as if to conceal her anxiety, but she was so tense that it turned into a grimace. "Why should you burden yourself with a kid, especially your sister's? You're tired enough of her already. There's a reason you live alone, and I swear I understand you where that's concerned. I'd give a lot to have only myself to take care of."

The night hadn't brought her any rest. She had rings under her eyes, and her mouth drooped a little. I remembered her as a teenager, looking at herself in the mirror for hours and miming kisses. She always said her lips were what the boys liked best about her. The best weapon to shoot them down with. In the meantime, she was the one who'd come down to earth.

"I asked you to give me time to think. Why don't you let me be the judge of what I want or don't want to do? Please sit down."

The air she'd kept in her lungs since I'd entered the room escaped in one go. She agreed to take a seat.

"You show up unexpectedly at my door. You give me a problem to solve and then solve it for me. You haven't changed since you were a kid, you're still like a tornado."

"Don't tell me you were ready to agree."

"And now you're doing my thinking for me. Better and better."

"It's just that . . . I need time. I was stupid to come here, and now I have to drive five hours back in the opposite direction. And when I get to Paris, I'll have to start looking again."

"And why would you find someone now, when you have even less time?"

"I'll manage."

"The way you manage with jobs? Or with men?"

"You bastard."

I sustained her gaze. I knew perfectly well what she was thinking at that moment. That I was really terrible. I shook the coffee machine and it immediately started working again. I filled two cups.

"You came into my territory. You're asking me to do something for you, so accept responsibility, for God's sake."

"What did you mean when you called me a tornado?"

"Don't you remember? It was your technique. You fooled everyone like that. As soon as you got home, you'd throw our parents a bone, an amusing anecdote or a good grade, which was impossible to check. And by the time they realized, you were gone again."

All at once, her face lit up. For a few seconds she was fifteen again. She made that pout that meant that she always got by, and then she returned to her body in the present.

"The first thing you noticed was that he didn't say hello. You won't be able to stand the fact that he never looks you in the eyes."

"He also patronizes me, you can add that too."

"Did he patronize you?"

"Last night, he told me I was afraid of playing chess, but that he could teach me."

"He spoke to you last night?"

"Yes."

"He doesn't usually speak to people so soon."

"That's very flattering. But tell him not to force himself. I like silence."

"Are you telling me you're going to keep him?"

"Possibly. I don't give a damn if he won't look me in the eyes or thinks I'm a fool. I have no intention of becoming friends with him. As long as he listens to me."

"If you decide on something, he'll do it, I told you. He doesn't like conflict."

"I'll take him to the field. After all, he's the same age as my boys."

"No, that one you can forget."

"Why?"

"He doesn't like sports."

"We'll see."

"When he doesn't like something, he doesn't usually change his mind. But you can leave him in his room. He never gets bored."

"Does he play chess all day?"

"He plays, and then he sleeps. Or else he makes notes in his exercise notebooks. He has lots of exercise books where he writes down possible moves."

"He's unusual, isn't he?"

"No more than kids who play video games."

"Ten days, not a day more. If you don't keep to the contract, I'll stick him on a train for Paris and you can figure something out when he gets there."

She drank her coffee in quick little gulps. She should have been a bit more relaxed by now, but she just couldn't manage it. She had to plan her day, the route she was going to take, everything that was at stake in her training course, and beyond that the job interviews, all the obstacles she had to get through and the others that were sure to arise. There were two buttons missing on her raincoat. The threads were still hanging. I was sure she hadn't told me everything about the situation, but at that moment I really didn't want to know anything more.

"If that's how it is, I'll wake him and talk to him."

We sat there in the kitchen, facing each other. I sensed that this moment would have consequences.

"What are you thinking?" she asked.

I didn't reply. I had no desire to share my thoughts with her. I wondered what our childhood would have been like if we'd lived through even one situation like this, where the distance between people was reduced out of necessity.

"You know, he really won't be any trouble to you if you leave him at home," she said.

"I believe you. But I'm taking him to the field anyway."

9

Madeleine drove me to the garage so that I could pick up my car, and when we got back she went and woke her son and told him he was staying with me.

Soon afterwards, I saw the boy walk his mother to the door. She gave him a kiss, which he didn't seem to want. It was all over, without a word, without any particular emotion.

I suggested breakfast to Léonard, and he filled a bowl full of cereal and took it to his room. I left him alone for at least an hour, then told him I'd decided to take him to training. He didn't show any surprise, or disapproval—no enthusiasm either, of course. He simply asked me when exactly I was planning to leave, which seemed to matter more to him than what had just happened, his mother's departure, the fact that he'd be staying in this house with his uncle who was a complete stranger. I told him we'd be leaving at nine-thirty and then went to take a shower. When I came out of the bathroom, Léonard was waiting under the clock in the hall. It was nine thirty-two and something seemed to be disturbing him. He was walking around in circles. He seemed worried. I pretended not to pay any attention to his little game, and we left the house a few minutes later.

He got in the front and I started the car. I had no intention of having a conversation with him during the ride. I'd always found it ridiculous the way adults tried to win children over by asking them questions about school, their friends, or what they wanted to do later in life.

When we got to the stadium parking lot, my boys were just going into the locker rooms. Two or three were lagging behind, as usual, and they looked insistently at the passenger I had with me. I thought I should have a word with them about my mysterious companion. Just tell them the truth, without going into details.

Léonard got out of the car. There was a bit of wind and he wrinkled his nose. I had the impression that all that space disturbed him more than anything else, and I remembered what my sister had said, that more than anything he loved staying in his room, sleeping and playing chess.

"You can sit there," I said.

I pointed to the stands and Léonard immediately headed for them and sat down at the end of the first row of benches.

Training a group of young people had taught me a fair amount about behavior and, even though he seemed so unusual, Léonard wasn't so different than a certain kind of player. The kind you must never force, the kind who'll come onto the field of their own accord, or never. That's why my idea was to let him watch a training session and see how he reacted.

The boys came out of the locker room in no particular order. I saw that Marfaing wasn't there, and neither was Hamed. Every day, there were a few absentees. At least two. They all knew they had to run ten laps around the field to start with, and they hated that.

"Who's the guy with you, sir?"

"My sister's son. She asked me to keep him during her vacation."

"Are you babysitting, sir?"

"If you like."

"It's weird that you have a sister!"

"Why?"

"Dunno, it's just weird. Doesn't he play soccer?"

"We'll see. Right, we're going to work on corner kicks today, and I want to see discipline and aggressiveness."

"We'll crack a few heads, sir, promise."

"Just crack the net, Bensaid."

I glanced at the stands. Léonard was still sitting in the same place. I was too far away to be sure, but it looked as if he was watching.

I divided the boys between attack and defense in front of the least damaged goal, and chose Cosmin to take the corner kicks. Of all of them, he was the one with the greatest potential. He was capable of wrong-footing an opponent and placing the ball on the head of a teammate from thirty yards. His one problem was that he didn't know whether it was really worthwhile spending fifteen years running around a soccer field, with all the uncertainties and risks that involved, when he could easily take the much less tiring option of following in his father's footsteps and running the bar opposite the railroad station.

The session started. Cosmin took some time to settle, because the ball was heavy and the wind that had swept away the rain was blowing slantwise. Two or three balls went way over their heads, another was much too off-center, and predictably that loudmouth Hervalet yelled that he never got the ball. Cosmin of course responded by giving him the regulation finger, and Bensaid, who was Hervalet's pal, joined in. Within two minutes, it was like the Gaza Strip. I used the whistle and announced that we'd drop the corner kicks and play a match on half the field.

"The first team to score three goals wins. If I see one of you heading straight for the goal all by himself, I'll send him off. If anyone else tries a between-the-legs pass instead of looking for back-up, I'll send him off too, I want a structured, properly thought-out game, is that understood?"

I went back to the touchline. I was looking down at the

ground as I walked, and thinking hard. I still had a few weeks before the beginning of the championship and I really didn't think I had a team. I looked up at the stands. The bench was empty.

I walked to the other side of the building. I told myself that Léonard couldn't be far away, but there was nobody there either. I looked all around. Nobody. I thought I had the situation under control, but maybe I'd been wrong all down the line! What if, beneath his impassive exterior, Léonard had been playing his cards close to his chest? What if he hadn't really accepted his mother's departure? Maybe it had stuck in his throat, and now he'd run away without even knowing where he was going, just to show his anger with adults who didn't understand.

I carried on to the edge of the ground and the sports complex. Nothing, no trace of the boy. A thought occurred to me. He might be in the car. In fact that was the most plausible explanation. He'd felt cold and taken shelter there. Like when he'd waited for my sister to come and get him, that first evening. Hadn't she told me he loved sitting it in all by himself? I walked straight to the parking lot, hoping I was right, but he wasn't there either. Above all, I mustn't panic. I needed a vantage point from which I could get a wider view of the surrounding area, and I decided on the stands. From up there, I had a chance of spotting him even if he'd gone and taken refuge over by the cemetery. I walked over to the bleachers and started climbing. And almost immediately, I stopped.

There was Léonard, lying on the ground between two rows of seats. That was why I hadn't seen him. He hadn't run away. He'd fallen asleep.

10

I sent everyone to the showers. The score stood at two all, and Bensaid protested, convinced that his team could still win. He was clearly the only one.

In the meantime, Léonard had shut himself in the car. I walked around the hood, sat down at the wheel, and set off. Léonard had put his head against the window and was looking sideways at the road as it drifted past. I had no intention of asking him what he'd thought of the training session. He'd already given me his answer by falling asleep in the stands. We were halfway home, and not a single word had been uttered. I stopped at a grocery to buy something to go with pasta, and when I got back to the car Léonard hadn't changed position. I assumed he was asleep. We weren't very far from the house. The first street lamps came on.

"I don't like soccer," Léonard said. "It's too simplistic."

I heard again that odd, affected tone of voice, which was hard to believe came from a boy of thirteen.

"You say that because you haven't seen a real match."

"One of my mother's friends used to watch soccer on Sunday evenings."

"That was the French championship. It isn't a good example."

He'd sat up and was staring at the dotted line in the middle of the road, as if hypnotized by it.

I parked outside the house. Léonard got out first and stood by the door, waiting for me to open it. Before he could go to his room, I pointed to the couch facing the television.

"Sit down. I have something to show you."

I went down into the basement and opened the door of the windowless room that contained Robert Herbach's "treasure." Robert had been my chief instructor when I was training to be a coach. He'd been like a father to me, sometimes surly but always close, and since his retirement had coincided with the end of my course, he'd given me this priceless gift, by way of farewell: his collection of videocassettes.

I switched on the fluorescent light and walked down the narrow aisle. In his thirty-year career, Robert had built up a collection of videos that traced the history of soccer, no more no less, through the greatest matches. Some of these records were known to everyone, others were very rare. There were the finest feats, the most dramatic situations, the moments of grace, and the fiercest altercations, everything the game can produce when it rises above mediocrity. And quite apart from the fact that, for anyone who loved soccer, seeing those images was a source of intense emotion, the collection was a first-class teaching tool. I'd inherited that treasure and felt responsible for it. I'd been worried about the age of some of the cassettes and had converted them to DVD. I'd also categorized the matches by theme, in order to make it easier to access the information. Robert Herbach had died of cirrhosis two years after hanging up his boots, and I'd tried to make that heritage of his bear fruit. I might forget about the treasure for weeks on end, but I always went back to glean something from it. To be honest, my relationship with the collection varied. Sometimes I felt Robert's benevolent presence in it. But sometimes I found these wonders too overpowering, because they represented a superior form of the game that I'd never have access to.

I stood in front of the wall of DVDs. Ever since Léonard had uttered the word "simplistic" on the way back, to describe the kind of sport that soccer was, I'd had a match in mind. One that seemed an appropriate response to his verdict.

I moved the little stool closer. The Champions' League matches were on the top. There it was, the one I was looking for. I checked the label. Manchester United vs. Real Madrid. Champions' League quarter-final. 2003.

Léonard was waiting in the living room, sitting on the couch. He was doing some kind of relaxation exercise with his hands, but at high speed. I loaded the DVD in the player, switched on the TV and pressed Play.

"Watch this while I make us something to eat. Especially the first half."

I didn't try to catch his eye. By now I was getting used to his ways and knew he would pay attention. His hands had stopped moving.

I went into the kitchen and washed the leeks. I diced and blanched them for my favorite pasta dish. I heard the sounds of the match coming from the living room. I knew it by heart. I had time to take a shower. Through the wall, I could hear the drone of the commentator. The second half had just started. Zidane was about to pass to Roberto Carlos, who was running forward at top speed, and Carlos would cross it back to Ronaldo, who just had to knock the ball into the goal. I slipped on a clean sweat suit and put the water to boil. I laid two places, facing each other. While I was throwing the pasta into the boiling water, I realized that the game had finished and that Léonard had paused the DVD player.

I heard a slight noise behind me and turned. My nephew was sitting at the table. He had moved his plate in order not to sit directly opposite me.

"There are more combinations in this match," Léonard admitted. "They're executed with greater speed and precision too, but they're still quite predictable. It's like I said. Number 5 moves like the bishop and Number 11 like the knight. When 11 moves diagonally, 5 moves into the middle and always passes back to 11. 11 shoots, or else he again relies on 5 to get closer to the line and then shoots. Four times out of five, he shoots into the left-hand side of the goal but when the ball is given to him on his right foot."

I preferred to say nothing. I drained and served the pasta, and Léonard started wolfing it down in a way that contrasted with his affected way of speaking.

"But I want to see other matches. Do you have any more?"

"Quite a few, yes. But why continue if it's such a limited game?"

"I learned chess in a café where Ma often left me. There were lots of players. I used to watch. They weren't very good, but it was interesting all the same. I like to use my brain. It's what I like best."

He finished his portion of pasta in three mouthfuls. Then he stood up without asking me anything and went back to the living room to watch the second half.

I calmly finished my dish and looked at the time on the clock in the hall. It was nine o'clock. I went back to the video library and selected other matches, all from different World Cups. I brought back a pile of DVDs, at least six boxes, which I placed on the low table in the living room, while Léonard still had his eyes riveted to the screen.

"Don't go to bed too late."

"When I'm tired, I sleep."

"Yes, I noticed that."

11

I shut myself up in my room. I needed to feel at home. I settled some overdue bills, threw out some circulars, then waited for my sister to call. It was what we'd agreed, but when the call didn't come, I dialed her number. All I got was a message saying she couldn't be reached. I went to bed and read *L'Equipe*. It was the issue from two days earlier. I skimmed it quickly. I hadn't really missed anything. Items about doping, astronomical transfer fees, fixed matches. It struck me this was the kind of thing my boys read every day.

The Manchester United–Real Madrid match must have finished. There was silence from the living room. Then I heard the anthem from one of the World Cups. Léonard had started on the pile. I sank into sleep.

I woke at eight in the morning. I hadn't set the alarm, because training was always in the afternoon. Since I had nothing urgent to do, I lay in bed, letting my eyes wander along the crack in the ceiling and trying to get my thoughts in order. It was then that my cell phone started ringing. I checked the number on the screen. I'd never seen it before. I hated picking up and hearing those sales people who asked you if you were satisfied with your payment plan and then tried to get you to switch to a new option. I let it ring twice more, then remembered that my sister was having problems with her provider. I picked up at the last moment.

"Madeleine here. I'm calling from the phone of a girl I'm doing the course with, so I'm not going to stay on the line for a long time."

"You really should get a phone of your own."

"I'll sort that out. In the meantime, I'll give you my room-mate's number. She'll pass the message on if it's urgent. The course looks brilliant. The teachers are great. I have to go, it's not my phone, and we're going back into class in a minute."

"Léonard's fine."

"What?"

"I said, Léonard's fine."

"Did you take him to your training session?"

"Yes."

"And?"

I opened my mouth to answer, but just then we were cut off. Maybe it was a problem with reception, or maybe Madeleine had hung up.

Léonard was asleep on the couch. He must have just dropped off, as he always did. The pile of DVDs had vanished, he'd gotten through the whole of it, but that wasn't all. There were others on the table, at least twice as many, which he'd brought up from the basement himself. He must have spent the night watching them. I went to him. He was sleeping curled up, his head against his arm. My eyes came to rest on a school exercise book at the foot of the couch. I remembered what my sister had told me about these exercise books where he noted down possible chess moves. I bent down, picked it up, and leafed through it. Sure enough, the pages were filled with chess games. You could follow the movements of the pieces on the board, the attacks, the parries. It was quite impressive. And then I continued skimming through pages until I came to the last drawings. I frowned. I wasn't sure I understood. These were no longer chess pieces that were shown, but players on a field, and the ball was moving around between them according to a very specific tactic.

I sat down on the edge of the couch. I had to face the facts. Léonard had spent the night viewing a dizzyingly large number

of soccer actions. And he hadn't just watched them. He'd carefully noted down a whole lot of combinations and tactical patterns connected with this simplistic game called soccer.

I made breakfast and waited for Léonard to wake up. I had
my coffee, watching him as he lay there surrounded by the
piles of DVDs. This strange specimen was trying to reduce the
history of world soccer—nothing more, nothing less—to a few
drawings. I wondered if I should laugh in his face or take him
seriously. At last, he opened his eyes and saw the cornflakes on
the table. He stood up and filled a bowl.

"I saw what you drew in your exercise book."

He didn't answer, but started eating. I went and fetched the
exercise book, sat down next to Léonard, taking care not to
face him, and opened the book at one of the pages devoted to
soccer. There was a drawing of a backward pass after a successful overlap of a winger.

"You know, the most difficult thing in soccer isn't inventing
combinations, it's actually performing them on the field in real
time. You can take more cornflakes."

I turned another page. This time the drawing depicted a
kind of play typical of the Italian national team, *Gli Azzurri*.
The scorpion tactic. You draw your opponent to you, create
gaps in his lines, then hit him with a lightning counter-attack.

"If you understand what your opponent's going to do,"
Léonard said, looking down at his bowl, "it's easier to respond."

"You see soccer like chess, right?"

"Only simpler and more repetitive."

"I was forgetting."

"It's true."

"Even if it is, tell me one thing: if you were on the field,
what position would you play in?"

He started chewing more slowly. He was thinking. He was
looking at the plan he'd drawn, players facing the goal. Each
player had a number, corresponding to the ones he'd seen in

the videos. I wondered if he was going to answer my question. His face was more inscrutable than ever. He carefully scraped the bottom of his bowl, not leaving any of it, then his hand advanced toward the exercise book and his index finger printed to player number 1, there in the middle of the goal. The goalkeeper, of course. I should have thought of that. The final bastion. The player who defended the line and whose movements were closest to those of a chess piece.

12

What did I have to lose by trying Léonard in goal? Favelic was our goalkeeper by default, because he was really too limited with the ball at his feet, but every time he put on the gloves, he gave the impression he'd been sent to stand in the corner. I had surplus kit in the house, a whole bagful of it. I found a sweat suit, boots his size, a bit worn for sure, but still decent, and even gloves that ought to fit him. I put everything down on his bed. Léonard was looking out the window and didn't turn around. But I was starting to know him and I wasn't offended.

I got my bag ready and went out to my car, leaving the door open behind me. Just as I was putting the key in the ignition, Léonard came out of the house in his goalkeeper's gear.

We drove to the stadium. The weather had improved distinctly since the day before. The temperature had gone up by at least three degrees and the wind had fallen. These were much better conditions for the ball. As I pulled up in the parking lot, I saw three of my boys, Marfaing, Bousquet, and Rouverand, the striker. They immediately noticed that Léonard was in his outfit, and they started talking among themselves. Getting out of the car, I cut their speculations short.

"Léonard is going to play in goal."

"We're going to have Favelic under our feet," Marfaing said.

"You could play behind him, to make up for it."

"That's not cool, sir."

"I'm sure you're easily good enough to do it."

I saw Rouverand sizing Léonard up. Center forwards always look at goalkeepers in a rather special way. They know they'll eventually come face to face with them in the penalty box. Léonard went straight onto the field, as if nothing else existed: his teammates, or any other parameter. He really did cut a strange figure, with his head too heavy for his body, his disproportionate arms, and his distracted demeanor. He was a long way from the catlike types who usually make good goalkeepers. I wondered, for a split second, if this test was such a good idea. My nephew might end up with egg on his face in front of boys his own age who didn't mince words. I might be exposing him unnecessarily. But it was too late to turn back.

"What are we going to do, sir?" Bensaid asked.

Costes, Tibert, and Hervalet were missing. Every day, the list got longer. It was either sudden food poisoning or a scooter that hadn't started. Anything was a good excuse.

"We're going to work on one goal. Overlapping on the wings, and crosses."

I sent Bensaid onto the right wing and, on the other side, Mutu, the black pearl—that was what they'd nicknamed him in the locker room—who was amazingly fast but just couldn't seem to stop before the line, let alone cross correctly. Rouverand positioned himself in the middle of the strikers, with Cosmin to feed him balls—those two had their set patterns—and the others, Marfaing, Bousquet, and Hamed made up the defense. I gave my instructions with one eye on Léonard. He seemed light years away, on Jupiter at least. He was looking at his gloved hands, and moving his fingers as if they weren't his.

"I want clean play. I'm not interested in your marking at all costs, what matters is how the play is constructed. A successful overlap, a well-placed cross, a serious shot. I don't want random kicks. I want concentration. Come on! In your places!"

Bensaid took the ball on his wing, and came back at full speed. He outflanked that beanpole Marfaing, who was still asleep, with disconcerting ease, and looked for Cosmin, just as I'd asked. The ball arrived at the wrong speed and Cosmin had to catch it on his back, but he was technically adroit enough to control it, turn so that he was again directly in line with the goal, and rely on Rouverand. It was a classic one-two situation and Kevin played along with it. He kicked it away with the flat of his foot, between Hamed and Bousquet, and Cosmin found himself smack in the penalty area, the ball at his feet, alone in front of the goal.

Léonard had certainly been thrown in the deep end. His defense had abandoned him and he was alone facing Cosmin, who loved these one-on-ones. The outcome was a foregone conclusion. Cosmin was going to bring it home. He maneuvered perfectly, pretending to draw Léonard to the right, so that he could then open his left foot and land the ball on the opposite side. A classic and very effective move. I could already see the ball in the net. Except that Léonard didn't take the bait but moved to the right and caught the ball in his arms. I couldn't help smiling. That move must have corresponded to one of the drawings in his precious exercise book. It was well played, but he hadn't done anything special either. After all, it was one of the most frequently encountered situations between a goalkeeper and a striker, who only had a fraction of a second to decide between a lob, a forceful kick, or sending the ball in the opposite direction than the expected one, and my nephew had simply chosen the right option. It could have been chance.

"Give it to Mutu, Léonard!" I yelled.

Léonard seemed to wake up from a dream and threw the ball in the direction of the black peal. The way he moved was far from orthodox, but the ball reached its destination.

The second action made me sit up more than the first. Mutu kept the ball on his wing, got as close as possible to the goal, drawing the defenders to the side, then turned and passed to Rouverand, who was completely unmarked and was already preparing his shot. It wasn't the subtlest move, for sure, but when it was well executed, it was usually unstoppable, because it left the goalkeeper with only two choices: to stay on his line or venture out into the penalty area, at the risk of leaving the goal open. But Léonard didn't fall into the trap. Although only a few seconds earlier he had seemed out of touch with the game, staring into space, his arms down by his sides, he now placed himself directly in the path of the ball and all he had to do was lie down and grab it, while Rouverand looked on in a daze.

"Well played, Léo," Bousquet said.

I went back to the touchline. For someone who'd never played soccer, my nephew had been very lucky, but after all, he wasn't facing the future stars of Real Madrid, just the Sedan under-16s, so it was nothing to write home about.

It was only with the third action that I finally admitted that something special was happening. From the start, I could feel the tension. Rouverand hadn't liked his ball being snatched from him just as he was about to strike, that was for sure, and Cosmin had had time to ponder his unsuccessful encounter with this boy whose head was too big. Now they were going to show him. Bensaid moved closer to midfield to increase the numbers. He passed the ball to Cosmin, who went straight into his usual performance, drawing the whole defense after him, then with an accurate back heel he served Rouverand, who was now in an ideal position, with a clear field in front of him, a little to the right of the goal, less than ten yards. He was going to set the record straight. At first, I thought he was going to kick the ball hard, but no, he slowed down. He didn't just want to score, he wanted to show that little newcomer who the boss really was in the penalty area, he himself, Kevin Rouverand, the player that all the clubs in the first division, and maybe even the English, would soon be fighting over. He took all his time to open his right foot, as if he was going to place the ball in the side net, to the left of Léonard, and when he felt his opponent rising to the bait, he abruptly changed direction to get rid of him and find himself alone facing an empty goal. It was well-played, except that just as he was about to strike, Rouverand saw the ball get away from him once again. Léonard had pretended to be deceived by his fake move, but had remained alert and, with a sliding tackle, pushed the ball away at the last moment.

There was a great silence on the field. You could have heard a pin drop. Léonard had realized that Rouverand was opening his foot to the right to trick him, whereas Cosmin had made the same move for a different outcome. He had once again chosen the right option. Was it just luck? This was starting to be a lot of luck. Just then my cell phone vibrated in my pocket.

"It's your sister. Is this a bad time?"

"Go on."

"In the end I didn't go back to my roommate. It's in the middle of nowhere, this training course! Luckily I found another student who lives not far from here and has been kind enough to put me up."

"Madeleine, I'm in the middle of a training session."

"Oh . . . I wanted to apologize for this morning. I couldn't stay any longer on the line, you were telling me something about Léonard . . . "

"I was telling you he's fine."

"What's he been doing today?"

"Playing soccer."

"Really?"

Suddenly, I heard yelling on the field. A fight had just broken out. I couldn't see who it was between, but everybody seemed to have joined in.

"I have to hang up."

"I wanted to talk to you about something else."

"I'll call you back."

"It's urgent, Vincent."

"Tonight."

There was chaos in front of the goal. Costes and Mutu were trying to calm Rouverand, who was waving his arms about, trying to justify himself. Some distance from the group, Léonard was walking around in circles with his head in his hands.

"Sorry to say this, sir, but your nephew's gone too far."

"It's true, sir!"

"Not all at the same time. What did he do?"

"He told Kevin he didn't know how to play. That's worse than an insult!"

"So Kevin blew up, it's only natural."

"And he moved back, it was bad luck, sir!"

"He hit the post!"

"Your nephew's weird, sir."

"That's enough for today. Come on, off to the showers."

They walked quickly away, without further ado, especially Rouverand.

I walked up to Léonard, who was still going around in circles. I tried to stop him to see what was wrong with his head, but he pushed me away coldly. That was enough, I shouted, and he stopped dead. He was still holding the back of his head. I gently moved his hand away. It was covered in blood. There was a cut on his scalp at least two inches long.

13

I put a makeshift bandage on Léonard and we set off for the hospital. In a situation like that, any other kid would have shown some emotion, not him. Apart from his reluctance to have me touch him, he hadn't displayed either anger or fear since the incident. He'd gotten into the car when I'd asked him, and that was all. He sat up straight in his seat and looked out at the road, his face still expressionless.

"What did you tell the boy who hit you?"

"The truth. That's what I always do."

"What exactly did you say?"

"That he should have done a backspin."

"Why?

"Statistics. Out of every fifteen head-to-heads with the goal-keeper, seven turn into goals. Out of seven goals, I counted only one dribble, two feints, and four backspins. So you have to do a backspin. That's what I explained to him. It was to help him."

"That's what you told him?"

"Yes."

"To help him?"

"Yes."

"And you got those statistics from watching those matches last night?"

"Yes. I started putting the moves into categories. The head-to-heads, the crosses, the corner kicks, the one-twos. But I didn't finish."

"And for all these moves you established statistics of success?"

"Obviously."

"Is that the method you use when you play chess?"

"Of course. But it's much more difficult with chess. In chess, I know one thousand and forty-three variations. And I'm not a very good player. In soccer, for the moment, I've only counted about fifty."

"But you didn't view all the recordings. And I don't have all the possible moves on those DVDs."

"That's true. But I'm sure there are a lot less than in chess."

Ahead of me a van was moving at a snail's pace. The driver must have been trying to find his way, or else looking for somewhere to park, but he wasn't flashing any lights. So I changed down a gear, pulled out, and accelerated. I didn't look behind me, paid no attention to the double white lines, and was gripping the wheel more than I needed to. I really had to calm down.

"When Kevin's facing you, you know he's going to dribble?"

"Yes. It's easy. You have to look at the foot he has his weight on. If the tip of the foot is pointing outwards, he's getting ready to dribble. I saw that when I froze the image."

"So every time a player is going to dribble, the foot he has his weight on is turned out?"

"No, three times out of four. It's a calculated risk. There's no such thing as a no-risk situation. It's the same in chess."

I turned onto the beltway that bypassed the center of town. We passed rows of low-rise buildings, and the hospital loomed up in front of us. It was a fairly new building, and the entrance to the emergency department was still under construction. I parked as best I could, between a truck and an ambulance.

The glass door opened automatically and I found myself at the reception desk, filling in a form about a boy whose date of birth I didn't know. Then we waited, sitting on chairs, next to a man with a swollen face who stank of booze. Léonard had started beating his leg back and forth, faster and faster. I had already seen him react that way when he'd settled into the bedroom at home. A doctor came up to us and asked us to follow him. We entered a room where the equipment looked brand new, and the doctor pointed to a bench for Léonard to sit on. A nurse joined us.

"How did he get this?" the doctor asked, examining the cut.

"He hit a goal post."

"Well, it's quite a deep cut. And there's a lot of dirt in it." He started cleaning the wound. "It's going to sting a little, young man," he said to Léonard. "Then we're going to put some stitches in. It may be a bit painful. But I get the impression you're a brave boy . . . "

Léonard didn't reply and the doctor stood there for a moment, looking at him, then came over to the cabinet where the instruments he would need were. I was standing next to it.

"Does your son always look at people that way?"

"He's my nephew."

"I mean, he avoids eye contact."

"He's quite shy."

"His reaction to pain is also unusual."

"What do you mean?"

"Children are more or less capable of controlling themselves. But he doesn't seem to be hurting at all, or very little, which is different."

"What exactly are you trying to tell me?"

He must have been in his forties. He wasn't the kind of overworked greenhorn you sometimes come across in emergency departments. He chose a needle with care and put the thread in without hesitating.

"Would you mind if a colleague of mine examined him?"

"For what reason?"

"I have the impression he's in a state of shock."

"Because he's miles away."

"Miles away?"

"You have that impression because he's miles away. But that has nothing to do with shock. He's always like that."

"You know it's just routine . . . that kind of examination."

I had no particular reason to object. After all, he was in his area of expertise. When I was on the soccer field, I didn't like anyone disagreeing with my decisions.

He picked up his phone and talked to a colleague named Catherine. He spoke quite softly and I didn't quite catch what he was saying. I looked at Léonard. He was waiting, sitting on the bench, his face turned to the white wall. I thought about the thousand and forty-three possible moves in chess. Maybe he was going over them.

The doctor made the first stitch. His movements were quick and precise. He asked the nurse for pliers to tighten the thread. At that moment, a woman of about thirty-five came into the room. She must have been the colleague he'd sent for.

"Are you this boy's uncle?"

"Yes."

"Can I speak to you for a moment?"

Her voice was calm, her eyes clear. She motioned to me to follow her into the corridor. There was a lot of movement out there. And noise. We avoided a gurney on which an old man was waiting. She stopped a little farther on, near a column that allowed us a bit of peace and quiet.

"I'm Dr. Vandrecken. My specialty is child psychiatry. I'm going to run a few behavioral tests, nothing complicated. Family members aren't normally present. Please don't think we're trying to keep you out of the loop. It's simply been established that having someone close to him there may distract the patient. Of course we'll have a proper talk after the tests. It's my understanding that you've only known the child for a short time."

"That's right."

"What's his family situation?"

"He lives with my sister."

"What about his father?"

"He left when he was seven."

"And your sister has given him to you to look after."

"Just for a few days."

"All right. There's a waiting room on your right. This won't take long."

She went back into the room where Léonard was and I stood there in the middle of the corridor. I didn't feel like being seated. Or facing a gurney. I looked for the nearest exit.

14

The cool air did me good. I leaned back against a wall, not far from the access ramp. I took several deep breaths to try to get rid of the tension inside me. In the building opposite, an old woman was smoking at the window of her room. All at once, she threw away her cigarette and withdrew her head, then a nurse appeared and abruptly closed the window.

An emergency ambulance arrived, siren screaming, and pulled up outside the main entrance of the hospital. The doors opened and the paramedics got to work. The care with which they moved the body, their faces, their general demeanor left no doubt about the gravity of the situation. I thought about my father. About the day he went into hospital, almost certainly like that, and never came out again.

He'd been admitted to the teaching hospital in Toulouse after being freed from his car, which had rolled over onto the shoulder of the highway, near Montauban. What had happened? The theory that had prevailed was that he'd fallen asleep at the wheel, having absorbed all kinds of booze. He'd been taken out of the wreck with terrible fractures, worst of all with the back of his skull smashed in, and had died after three days in a coma, without ever waking up. I'd learned the news by telephone, from my sister. I remember how she'd hated my reaction, which was too cold for her taste: she herself had burst into tears. That was the day she first told me I had a heart of stone, which was fine by me. My father had ended up in a highway ditch, close to his destination. There hadn't been any obstacle in his path, any treacherous bend, any reckless driver picking a quarrel with him. He had been his only obstacle. His capacity for destruction, especially self-destruction.

"Monsieur Barteau?"

A voice drew me away from my thoughts. It was the child psychiatrist. She was standing against the light and I had to screw up my eyes to see her better.

"You know, Dr. Mérieux is an excellent doctor."

"Why are you telling me that?"

"Because a good doctor doesn't just rely on what he knows, he also uses his intuition. Have you ever heard of Asperger's syndrome?"

"No, never. Is it a disease?"

"Not exactly. It's a condition. A kind of mild autism that often produces exceptional people. Some great pianists have Asperger's. In all likelihood, Einstein did as well. Bobby Fischer, the world chess champion . . . "

"Top sportsmen?"

"Not as far as I know, but it's quite possible. What do you do for a living, Monsieur Barteau?"

"I'm a soccer coach."

"So you made him play soccer."

"That's not quite how it happened."

"Do you mind telling me?"

Things were going much too fast for me. I felt the need to regain control, or at least try. "Do you mind telling me where Léonard is?"

"Right now he's playing chess with Dr. Mérieux, and probably making a fool of him."

"I need a coffee."

"We can go to the cafeteria, as long as we sit outside. If I drink coffee, I have to smoke. It's bad, I know."

There were three tables on a little terrace. At one of them, a blind old man was sitting, smiling at God knows what. Dr. Vandrecken lit her cigarette and crossed her legs. Worried as I'd been about Léonard, I hadn't realized earlier what an attractive woman she was. But she didn't seem to attach any importance to that.

"You were telling me he's been playing soccer."

"We started out by saying that soccer was a simplistic game in comparison with chess."

"And that annoyed you."

"No, I think it's wrong, that's all. And since I have a video collection of the greatest matches, I gave him one to watch."

"To make him change his mind?"

"To help him form a more informed opinion."

It was obvious that Dr. Vandrecken was evaluating me at the same time as she was asking me questions about Léonard.

"I see. And what happened?"

"He watched the first match very attentively, then asked me for more. And then he went and helped himself from my video collection. In one night, he watched more than fifty, noting down the combinations, putting the moves into categories, calculating the probability of success depending on the players' decisions."

"He's applying what he knows about chess to soccer."

"Precisely. So I asked him what position he saw himself playing in if a soccer field was a chessboard."

"And he said goalkeeper."

"Did he tell you that?"

"No. But it's logical. A goalkeeper's movements are limited. His space easier to grasp. And so you took him to the field."

"Yes."

"And what happened?"

"What he did was quite amazing."

Having reached this point in the conversation, Catherine Vandrecken lit another cigarette. She was nodding her head slightly, clearly weighing up different ideas, trying to draw conclusions.

"You need to have some idea about Asperger's syndrome," she resumed, "or there's a chance you'll misinterpret things. An Asperger's sufferer doesn't see things the same way you and I do. That doesn't mean he or she is crazy or mentally defective. Quite the opposite. But an Asperger's sufferer really is different, and we have to be constantly aware of that."

"Give me some examples."

"His brain isn't constructed like ours. To oversimplify, we put our thoughts in boxes that are built into us during our first years of life and allow us to find our way. We take them for granted, we're no longer even aware of them, but thanks to them we're able to react in ways that are appropriate to the situations that crop up in our everyday lives. An Asperger's sufferer doesn't have those boxes. For genetic reasons, they aren't built into his brain, so he has to make them up as he goes along. At least if he wants to live in society. To put it very roughly, he's a Martian visiting earth. He's from another planet and doesn't understand anything about the way we function. He doesn't sleep like us. He doesn't like to be touched. He never tells lies. He speaks in a very pedantic way."

"That's Léonard."

"In these conditions, what can he do? Either he's himself, which means that he'll be misunderstood, rejected, sometimes mistreated. Or else he imitates us so as not to attract attention, to be left in peace, which is his main objective."

"How can he imitate us if he doesn't understand us?"

"By using his mental capacities, which gives him the possibility to observe, to classify, to memorize. He's forced to do that, since he isn't like us. He must constantly think, look for clues, use the information he has about us to figure out what he needs to do. It's tiring work, and that's why he suddenly drops off to sleep when this process drains him of his energy."

As Dr. Vandrecken went on with her explanations, I saw images pass by. Léonard's disturbing behavior was starting to make sense.

"Is Léonard playing soccer because he's afraid I'll reject him?"

"Partly. But it may also come from a more complex feeling."

"What kind of feeling?"

"It's apparently a game he's established with you. Asperger's sufferers take an interest in us if we don't act like idiots. Through soccer, he may have a relationship with you."

"At first he suggested we play a game of chess. But I can't play chess."

"So, since you can't go into his world, he comes into yours."

"Yes, at least in his way. I didn't ask him to cause havoc with my team."

"Is that what he did?"

"Pretty much."

"Part of him wants to copy, part of him refuses to . . . That's the real question for an Asperger's sufferer. Constructing his identity can be very painful. How's his relationship with his mother?"

I took my time replying. To me, that was by far the most complicated question. "I don't know. We don't see each other very often. She asked me to keep him because she had no other way out."

"She doesn't think there's anything unusual about her son?"

"No. He has his own personality. That's what she told me."

"She's in denial. It's very common. But for the child it's more complicated. He wants to please his mother, to behave in a—quote-unquote—normal manner, and, on the other hand, he can't help expressing his difference. You'll have to forgive me, but I must go. I have patients to see."

I stood up to say goodbye. She held out her hand. Then she looked in her pocket, probably for a card. Her pen fell out. I quickly picked it up. She smiled at me.

"Don't hesitate to call me. If I'm not in the hospital, the office will know where I can be reached."

15

I waited for Léonard by the car, leaning on the hood. If he was so intelligent, he could easily find me. He eventually came out of emergency and headed straight for me as if nothing had happened, walking in that slightly awkward way of his. He ran his hand through his hair. He could probably feel the stitches.

"I won both games," he said, coming level with me.

"Get in."

I drove out of the parking lot, my teeth clenched. And they stayed clenched until we were beyond the beltway and surrounded by traffic.

"Listen carefully, because I'm not going to repeat this. The first thing is that you don't have to play soccer. Nobody's forcing you. I'm not going to throw you out of the house or stop feeding you if you don't play. Play because you want to, and for no other reason. And I don't care if you don't look at me, but at least make a sign that you've understood."

There was a moment's silence in the car, then Léonard made a slight movement with his chin.

"The second thing is that you have a gift. Why or how doesn't matter. But it's a fact."

What followed was what I absolutely needed him to understand. I took my time choosing my words.

"The third thing is the most important. If you want to go back on the field, I have no objections, but there's one condition. You have to accept the rules of the group. You can't behave the way you did this afternoon. You don't talk like that to another player. You don't lecture him because you think you're better than him."

"I was trying to help him—"

"Shut up and listen. You weren't trying to help him, you just wanted to show him how much you know. You thought you were the teacher, but you're not. Just because you watch videos doesn't mean you're a good player. I want to see you move your chin."

"I don't have to, I can speak."

"Then speak."

"I understand what you're saying."

"That's fine, then."

We didn't exchange another word until we got home, and as soon as the door was open, Léonard went straight to his room. At dinnertime I suggested he eat, and he replied that he wasn't hungry. I didn't insist. If he felt peckish during the night, he knew where the refrigerator was. I advised him to take a shower and not go to bed too late. I didn't see him for the rest of the evening.

I liked being alone in my kitchen. I watched the news channel. A storm had ravaged the coast of Chile. Boston had beaten Miami at basketball. Unemployment had increased by two percentage points in the eurozone. I let the images drift by, but my mind started to wander. I thought about Catherine Vandrecken smoking her cigarette, her legs crossed, in the cafeteria of the hospital. Suddenly, my phone started vibrating. I'd forgotten my sister was supposed to call. This time the number was withheld. She'd changed phones again.

"Vincent, it's me. Can you hear me?"

"Very well."

"I couldn't call you before, the days are really busy, and we have homework to do in the evening. Luckily, Patrice is helping me out, I don't know how I'd manage without—"

"Who's Patrice?"

"I told you about him. He's the guy who's putting me up."

"Now he's putting you up."

"Don't you ever listen? I told you—"

"I thought it was for one night."

"We get on really well, we're staying together. He's going to open a bar in Châteauroux. He has these great ideas for ensuring customer loyalty. He wants to invite creative people, celebrities, you should see the contacts he has. And don't go crazy, but he'd like me to be in on it with him!"

"You mean he wants money from you."

"Vincent, that's not funny. It's a terrific proposition. He doesn't need my money, he's rolling in it. It's because we both have a feel for these things. He doesn't just want me to work for him as a waitress. He wants us to be partners, don't you see?"

"And what exactly is he asking you for?"

"Twenty thousand, I mean, come on, that's nothing at all for a deal like this."

"Luckily, you don't have it."

"What? I can't quite hear you."

"I said, luckily you don't have it."

"Well, listen to this. I talked to my bank about consumer credit."

"I thought you were in the red."

"That's just it, it'll pay off the overdraft and still leave me fifteen thousand! We only have the paperwork to do, and I'll have the money next week. Then all I'll need is five thousand. That's what I wanted to talk to you about. It'd only be for a few weeks. As soon as the business is launched . . . "

I felt the need to sit down. Even though I knew her, she could still amaze me. I was torn between wanting to laugh, hang up, or scream, but I knew I absolutely mustn't let my emotions get the better of me. I had to keep my eyes wide open when she was doing one of her conjuring tricks. I had to ask the right questions.

"So now you're asking me for five thousand, is that right?"

"I'll pay it back with interest, if you like."

"That's not the point. You've known this guy for a couple of days. Don't you think you should wait a while and see—"

"Vincent, you don't get it. This is my big break!"

"We can talk about it when I see you. You're still coming for your son a week from Sunday, aren't you?"

"Of course."

"Don't you want to speak to him?"

"Oh, you know, he never says anything on the phone, it freaks him out more than anything."

"It's up to you."

"Are you having any problems with him?"

I couldn't see myself explaining over the phone what had led to that incident on the field, let alone mentioning the conversation with Catherine Vandrecken. I needed to have her in front of me to talk about that.

"Everything's fine."

"This soccer thing, is it for real?"

"He tried anyway. Whether he'll continue is another matter."

"I still can't believe it."

16

By 8:45 A.M., Léonard was under the clock in the hall, waiting to go. He'd had his breakfast, washed his bowl, put on his sweat suit, and was ready. I was also getting ready, but slowly, and the closer the minute hand got to nine o'clock, the more stressed my nephew seemed.

I closed the door at two minutes to nine, and didn't say anything until we were in the Peugeot, but once on board I felt the need to send him a message.

"In my world, you can be five minutes late."

He'd already put on his gloves as if he wanted to be ready to dive for a ball as soon as he got out of the car. He was making repetitive movements with his fingers.

There was fog in the parking lot. I asked Léonard to wait for me. I had to talk to the others. We couldn't just carry on as if nothing had happened. I walked down the corridor, which bore witness to how dilapidated the facilities were. Patches had come away from the walls in places, but at least there was light, which wasn't the case everywhere. I heard the boys through the wall. They were letting off steam, ribbing each other and letting out war cries. I went into the locker room and they almost immediately fell silent.

"Today we're going to have a little match."

"Great, sir!"

They saw matches as just another opportunity to let off steam. Which meant I still had a lot of work to do.

"Don't get carried away. This isn't playtime. What I want

before anything else is for you to apply in a game situation the tactics you learned in the technical classes. Individual feats, assuming you're capable of them, are for a later stage. I want to be able to evaluate your ability to carry out instructions. A tactical approach, agreed?"

They groaned and started heading for the exit.

"I haven't finished!"

I looked for Rouverand. He was usually the first out on the field, but now he was behind his teammates.

"Léonard will be with us again for this session. Yesterday's incident is closed. I've reminded him of certain rules of teamwork. He has to get used to it because he's a bit of a loner. But I also ask you to respect him. The way he reacts may surprise you, but let me be the judge of his ability to fit in or not."

"He's a good goalkeeper, sir."

"That's all we care about. We don't give a shit about the rest!"

"That's right, sir."

"Then get out there."

They rushed into the corridor. By now the fog had lifted, but the ground was still damp. I put Rouverand and Léonard in the same team. I was in no hurry to see them facing up to each other again. The match started. I took up position on the touchline. Of course, I intended to supervise all the players, but I'd be lying if I didn't admit that I was focusing my attention on my nephew's behavior. So far he'd only been involved in play situations that were limited in space, corner kicks, attacks on a single goal. A match, however modest, involved seeing if he was capable of reacting on another level.

The answer to my questions wasn't long in coming. At the first onslaught from the other team, he came to the edge of his eighteen yards, just as an experienced goalkeeper would have done, and got the ball away from Bousquet, who'd gotten past the defense and was almost offside. And with the subsequent corner kick, the demonstration was even more striking. He grabbed hold of the ball from the middle of a cluster of players, without any strain, as if he'd gone in to pick flowers.

What made it all the more spectacular was that he clearly didn't have either the muscle tone or the usual physical resistance of a young player his age. To be honest, he gave an impression of slowness, even sluggishness. Most of the time, his arms hung down by his sides, as if he didn't know what he was supposed to do. He walked more often than he ran. He wasn't particularly skillful and his attention seemed very relative.

So how did he do it? Everything rested on his reading of the game. On high-flying balls, he wasn't conspicuous for his quick reflexes, but he jumped at just the right moment, and that more than made up for it. On his goal line, he moved quite slowly, but he started moving so early that he cut off the path of the ball and rarely found himself caught out. To sum up, he seemed asleep, but he was always there for the ball, and all because of his exceptional reading of the game, that chessboard he had in his brain where the players moved according to calculated probabilities in order to make moves that were actually quite predictable, even though they themselves didn't know it.

After an interception that quickly turned into a counterattack, Rouverand scored. While he and his teammates celebrated, Léonard stayed in his net, his face as expressionless as usual. But that peculiarity of his had already ceased to be a problem. I realized that by observing the reactions of his teammates. They turned to him and raised their thumbs, without trying to drag him into their celebrations. He was different, he was even a little strange, but his effectiveness was staring to give them a good feeling. This weirdo was their goalkeeper. Soon they wouldn't want any other.

The irony wasn't lost on me. What every coach dreams of

finding, a little soccer genius, I had right there in front of me, revealing his skills, and all because my sister was in trouble and couldn't find any way out except to ask me, her brother, to look after her kid. But it couldn't be so easy. Léonard must have an Achilles heel. The subterfuge was sure to be discovered sooner or later. A winger wasn't a knight, nor was a center-forward a bishop.

Just as I was venturing this doubt, Bensaid blocked the ball in midfield and gave it to Mutu straight down the middle. In a few strides, the black pearl justified his reputation as an eater-up of space and ended up in the eighteen-yard box, and moving at top speed. What could Léonard be thinking at that moment? What situation was he going to relate this face-off to among the dozens of scenarios stored in his impressive memory? But before the answer could materialize, Marfaing came back from nowhere to bring down Mutu rather too aggressively. I ran onto the field to prevent any altercation, but the foul was so blatant that nobody questioned it, not even the culprit, and I pointed at the penalty spot while the others regrouped out of the area to watch the show.

Mutu decided to get his own back, and as far as for everyone was concerned it was a forgone conclusion. Léonard would draw the ball to him like a magnet, and Mutu would demonstrate once again that even though he was a terrific runner, he couldn't be relied on to deliver the knockout blow. But that wasn't at all what happened. Mutu ran forward, for sure, and as everyone was expecting, he produced a perfectly unremarkable shot, whose one merit was that it was well lined up, and it was now that Léonard's Achilles heel became blindingly obvious. While all the other players watched, he stayed on his line, unable to react to this undistinguished ball, which rolled into the goal and slowly died in the net.

It was so absurd, so unthinkable, that the boys didn't even laugh. They stood there struck dumb with surprise, while in a flash, I saw again the piles of DVDs, and the explanation for this fiasco became clear. In all those treasures, as luck—bad luck—would have it, there had been no penalties. My nephew had quite simply had no point of reference for the moment when Mutu had run forward, and he'd simply gone into shutdown.

17

Léonard moved away from the goal, walking at first, then, when I called to him, he started running. The only thing he wanted was to disappear. I set off after him. He had edged his way into the bushes at the edge of the stadium before I could catch up with him, and I had a terrible time getting him out. He'd tried to push through the vegetation, but the thorns had snagged him and gradually he'd gotten tangled up. Now he'd stopped moving. I slowly went to him, freed him from the briars, and walked him back to the car.

When we got home, I led him straight to the bathroom. The thorns had scratched his face and hands. I disinfected his abrasions. I expected him to reject this contact, but surprisingly he let me, as if he'd lost the strength to resist. When I'd finished, he went back to his room without a word, shut the door behind him, and I realized I had to leave him alone. That was all he was asking of me.

I spent a long time in the living room, staring at the DVDs scattered on the table and thinking. I remembered then that Catherine Vandrecken had said I could call her if I needed help. I took her card and dialed the number of the child psychiatry department. I was put on hold, then finally told that Dr. Vandrecken was seeing patients and couldn't be reached. I decided to go to the hospital without waiting. I had the feeling I'd been playing sorcerer's apprentice, that I'd let myself be overcome by the exciting prospect of discovering a champion. But he was just a kid. And he'd been humiliated.

I left a note in the kitchen in case Léonard came out of his room, but I strongly doubted it. He was exhausted and would sleep for hours. I didn't say in my note that I was going back to the hospital. I claimed I had shopping to do. But I emphasized the essential point: he was home and nobody here could harm him.

There were already a few people in Dr. Vandrecken's waiting room, including an exhausted-looking young couple with their child in their arms and a woman in her forties with her son, who must have been about Léonard's age and was trying to attract her attention away from sending texts on her cell phone. The couple's turn came, they were in the consulting room for almost forty-five minutes, and I told myself the woman and her child would get the same amount of time, but barely fifteen minutes later the secretary told me to go in, and I found myself face to face with Catherine Vandrecken. Unsettled, I searched for words to explain why I'd come.

"Good to see you again. How's Léonard?"

"Some . . . things have happened."

"What kind of things?"

"He wanted to continue going to the stadium. I left the choice up to him. I told him he had to do it for himself."

"You told him that?"

"Yes."

"That's very good. So what happened?"

I started telling her how brilliant Léonard had been, thanks to his viewing of the videos, his ability to memorize and reproduce play situations, but also how he'd been paralyzed, unable to block a ridiculously poor penalty kick because his brain had nothing to relate it to. Catherine Vandrecken heard me out, and remained silent well after I had finished my story. She looked grave, but then she smiled. It's incredible how good that smile made me feel.

"You remember what I told you about the boxes. He didn't have a box corresponding to penalties. He has to construct it."

"I realized that. But after the penalties, there'll be another missing box. It'll never end."

"How did he react after he let the ball through?"

"He went and hid in the bramble bushes. I took him back to the house, he went to his room, and now he wants to be alone."

"Because he's ashamed. It's his shame we have to work on. When you say he'll always be missing boxes, it's true, but each time he agrees to construct a new one, he'll gain self-confidence. He'll prove to himself that he can get over the shame, and gradually the shame will disappear."

"Do you really believe that?"

"I know how you're feeling. You're wondering if it's worth dragging him into a world that has so many obstacles . . . and what right you have to do that."

"Precisely. He's happy when he plays chess."

"How about giving me a lift to the theater?"

"I beg your pardon?"

"I'm supposed to meet some friends. The show starts at six o'clock, and I wasn't meant to see any more patients."

"I'm sorry, I tried to reach you by phone, but—"

"You were right to come. In fact, it was important that you did. If you drop me at the theater, we can still talk a little on the way."

She stood up without waiting for an answer, as if taking it for granted. She took off her white coat. She was wearing a simple black dress underneath. I helped her on with her coat. It was a strange situation. I'd come to ask her advice, and now we were almost like a couple going out on the town. Except that I was nowhere near as smartly dressed as she was.

Catherine Vandrecken got in my car and we drove toward the center. She continued the conversation as if everything was normal. She was behaving as if we'd known each other for a long time.

"You say he's happy when he plays chess. He really ought to have a partner, which can't happen very often. Most of the time he plays alone, doesn't he?"

"That's true, but he likes being alone."

"Of course. But he also needs other people. It's just a matter of balance. In that way, he's not so different from neurotypicals."

"Neurotypicals?"

"The people we call normal. You and me. I'm sure the reason he took an interest in soccer wasn't just to have a relationship with you, but also to play with other boys his own age."

"He doesn't factor them in."

"Oh, but he does. When he's ashamed, it's partly because of them, and when he's proud it's also partly because of them. Try to get away from the obvious patterns. Just because someone doesn't speak, it doesn't mean he can't communicate. And just because he won't look people in the face, it doesn't mean he's ignoring them. Actually, he shares one thing with us, even though it's on another level. He needs to be himself, but he also needs to have relationships with others. If he can find a place on the soccer field, and be recognized for what he is, it'll be fantastic for him."

"What if he fails?"

"Why should he fail? You're going to help him."

"You overestimate me. I saw a chance to recruit a good goalkeeper, that's all."

"I don't believe you."

We came to Place de Verdun, where the municipal theater was. The audience was starting to go in. I parked half off, half on the sidewalk.

"I'll leave you here."

"No, you have to stay with me to the end."

For the second time, she didn't leave me any choice. She took my arm and drew me to the foot of the steps. Her friends were equally well dressed. There were two of them, and they looked like mother and daughter. They looked at me in what seemed an amused way. But maybe I was being a bit paranoid.

"Let me introduce Vincent, who was kind enough to drive me here."

I said hello to the two women and got away as soon as I could. Getting back in my car, I glanced at the theater. There was almost nobody left in the square in front of it. Catherine Vandrecken was at the top of the steps. I could have sworn she was looking in my direction.

18

I walked into the house. It was silent and dark. I switched the lights on in the corridor and went straight to the kitchen. My note was still on the table: clearly, Léonard hadn't left his room while I was away. I thought for a moment. What Catherine Vandrecken had told me had been going around and around in my mind on the drive home. It was the kind of moment of decision you get in the locker room. You don't have much time. There are lots of unknowns. You have to choose one option and believe in it. The worst thing, always, is to do nothing.

I went to Léonard's room. The door was shut. I put my hand on the handle. It was the point of no return. Léonard was sitting on the bed. He had his back to me. He was looking straight ahead, his shoulders slumped, his head a little tilted.

"I think if I have a look," I began, "I should be able to find a video of penalties. But if you really want to play, that won't be enough. You must be able to react even when you don't have anything to relate it to. Otherwise, I'll never be able to put you into a real match. And that'd be a pity because you're very good. I really think that. So do your teammates. You saw it for yourself, they didn't make fun of you when you missed that penalty. They were surprised, that's all. You think they would have let you off that easily if they didn't respect you?"

Léonard slowly raised his head. He kept his back to me, but I knew he was paying attention.

"Now, nobody's forcing you to play, especially not me. But

if you want to continue, we can think about a method. Every player has a weakness, and it's often the thing that becomes his strength. Zidane was slow. That slowness made it necessary for him to develop his vision of the game, and he realized that the ball would always go faster than his legs. He became the greatest passer of all time. I can train you to expect the unexpected. But it's impossible if you don't want it. So it's up to you. Now I'm going to make something to eat."

I took a pizza from the freezer and put it in the oven. I had time to take a shower. I saw my face in the mirror and it struck me that I really needed a shave. This was the man whose arm Catherine Vandrecken had taken to go to the theater. That didn't make any sense.

When I came out of the bathroom, Léonard was already in the kitchen looking for the flatware. It wasn't an obvious thing for him to do, because since he'd been here, I'd always laid the table, whether for breakfast or for dinner. I didn't want to interfere because I thought he was responding, in his way, to the proposition I'd made him in his room: to tackle the unexpected. I sensed from a distance that he was making an enormous effort to open the drawers without knowing what they contained, that what for any other kid would have been curiosity was for him a source of anxiety. I went and changed in order to be more comfortable, but also to avoid my presence embarrassing him even more. I put on an old sweat suit, one that I couldn't bring myself to throw away even though it had quite a few holes in it.

By the time I got back to the kitchen, the table was laid. Léonard had solved the brain teaser, which was what finding the flatware, the napkins, the glasses, and everything needed for the meal must have been for him. But he'd done more than that. He'd arranged the plates in such a way that we could have dinner facing each other. I took the pizza out of the oven and cut it into slices. It was a simple meal, which suited both of us.

"If you like, once we finish eating we can watch a penalty shootout that's gone down in soccer history. It's the one in the final of the Superclásico between Brazil and Argentina at the Buenos Aires stadium in 2012."

Léonard was listening. He had a slice of pizza in his hands and was slowly chewing. His eyes were fixed on an imaginary point to the right of me, but I was used to this peculiar manner of his by now, and it didn't disturb me anymore.

"The radio was broadcasting the match live, the television interrupted its programs to give priority to what was happening. Taxes stopped. People swarmed into cafés that had a TV or radio. The ground floors of apartment buildings, too. The whole city went crazy."

That was when he raised his head a little and his eyes came to rest on me. "Who won in the end?"

I was so surprised, I paused for a moment. His face was still that enigmatic mask I knew, but his eyes met mine, at least for two or three seconds; it felt like an eternity.

"Brazil," I replied.

19

There was no group training scheduled for the next day. It was perfect for what I was planning to do. Mid-morning, I loaded in the car all the balls I had in reserve and took Léonard to the field to practice penalties. Just him and me. There was no wind that day, and not a cloud in the sky. It was cold but dry. We walked across the thick turf to the goal. Léonard took possession of his line. I placed a ball on the penalty spot, and moved back to explain a few things to my nephew.

"Why is a penalty a complicated exercise for the goalkeeper? Because it's more difficult to guess where the striker will put the ball than in open play. During a match, the player is usually running when he shoots, he's bound by his own momentum and has to make a rapid decision, which makes it harder for him to conceal his intentions. In the case of a penalty, it's different. The player is still, he can do a short run-up, start when he wants, choose his angle at the last moment, and he has both sides of the goal as possibilities."

Léonard was staring at his hands as he listened to me, stretching his fingers as wide as they would go.

"So the best way you have of guessing where the ball is coming from during a penalty isn't to watch the striker, who can easily trick you by his manner, but to focus your attention on the ball. In tennis, they say the good players see the ball leave their opponent's racket. If they wait until it's come over the net to see where it's going, it's too late. Well, it's the same thing with penalties. Watch the ball leave the foot. Concentrate on that. In the first three yards the ball covers, you have to figure out where it'll go. Afterwards, it's too late. Now, let's get down to it."

I took three steps as a run-up. I made sure that Léonard was ready. Then I placed the ball in the right of the net, with the flat of my foot. It wasn't a strong kick, and the ball didn't go very close to the post, but Léonard let it in without reacting.

"If the ball goes into the net, it's no big deal. Concentrate on its trajectory!"

I shot a second ball and it hit the other side of the net. It went in just as easily, but this time Léonard took his head in his hands.

"Don't be afraid of looking ridiculous. There's only you and me here."

For the third shot, Léonard bent his knees and opened his arms wide. He really wanted to try something. When I shot, he advanced toward the ball and this time he grazed it. But when he saw it in the net, he moved away from the goal and started walking around in circles.

"A very good goalkeeper only stops one penalty in five. You just have to keep going. You'll stop one in the end."

These words made him react. He stopped dead and turned to me. "If you lost ten games of chess, I'm sure you'd stop. But you know the solution. Don't play."

I took the remark on board. "Okay. I'm going to start playing chess. Just give me a bit of time to learn."

"I'll beat you hands down."

"It doesn't matter."

"You'll play even if you always lose?"

"Of course. Until I win a game."

"It'll never happen."

He stood there for a moment longer, then went back to the goal, and the penalty session resumed. It took fourteen before he stopped one. He lay down on top of the ball and hugged it for a very long time. Then he started losing again, but his body had relaxed. He took chances, daring to move to one side, or taking two steps forward in order to reduce the angle. He blocked another shot, a more difficult one this time.

"Someone's watching us," he said.

I turned toward the stands. A woman was sitting at the end of one of the benches. I recognized her. It was Catherine Vandrecken.

We resumed our practice session. Léonard stopped a third penalty, a ball that went under the bar, and then all the others went in. He had been staring at the ball for so long, he was suffering from nervous exhaustion. He was almost swaying. I signaled to him that the session was over, and we collected the balls. Catherine was waiting for us on the touchline.

"Have you been here for a long time?"

"A while."

"You were lucky to find us, there isn't usually any training today."

"It's my day off. You could invite me to lunch if you like. Not to a restaurant, your place, it doesn't have to be grand."

This woman had the gift of catching me off guard. I looked for a way of getting out of it.

"I'm sorry, but my fridge is empty."

"I'll take care of everything. Do you like Vietnamese?"

20

We stopped on the way. Accompanied by Léonard, Catherine Vandrecken literally plundered an Asian delicatessen. It was a no-parking zone, and I stayed in the car. I had plenty of time to watch her as she pointed to what she wanted to buy. She was wearing a turtleneck sweater and pants. She was a different person than the doctor at that moment. They both got back in the car, as excited as if they'd left without paying.

When we got home, I warmed up the containers and Léonard laid the table. He hardly hesitated. Compared with a penalty, it was easy. Catherine sat down at the table, without waiting for us, and started jabbing at one of the dishes.

"Sorry if I'm rude, but I'm very hungry."

Léonard, who was bringing water in a jug, suddenly froze. "You took my seat," he said in a very serious voice.

"Léonard, there are no allocated seats."

"No, he's quite right," Catherine said, and moved.

Léonard got his usual seat back and Catherine continued eating.

"When I was a child," she said, "I had my seat at the corner of the table, to the right of my father, and wouldn't have changed it for the anything in the world. Whenever friends of my parents were invited over, I'd sit down at the table, sometimes half an hour before the meal, to be sure that nobody would take my seat. Even now, I have my favorite seat in the hospital canteen, right at the back, the last chair next to the window. If it isn't free, I get upset, and, depending on my mood, I can even go so far as to take my tray to my office, rather than sit somewhere else."

Catherine turned to Léonard and pointed to me with the tip of her chopstick.

"This man says there are no allocated seats, but I'm sure he has his habits and doesn't like departing from them."

By the time I took the spring rolls from the oven, my nephew had started speaking, and it was as if nothing could stop him.

"He puts his bag down in the hall before leaving for training, always in the same place, under the clock. Then he goes around the house, turns off the water, and picks up his bag again. In the evening when he comes back, he puts on a sweat suit with holes in it, always the same one . . . "

"Léonard, this is of no interest to anyone."

"I don't agree. Go on, Léonard."

"He has three toothbrushes, but only uses one."

"Are you done yet?"

"When he goes to his car, he always walks in front of the hood, never behind."

"I've never even noticed . . . "

"Always in front of the hood, I checked. And when he laces his shoes, he always starts with the left. Never the right."

"Have you been spying on me?"

"He's just very observant, that's a great quality. Aren't you going to sit down?"

I joined them. All three of us forgot about the plates, and ate straight from the containers. Catherine asked me to explain to her what offside meant in soccer. The anesthesiologist in her department was a supporter of Paris Saint-Germain, and every Monday morning he'd tell her about the achievements or disappointments of his favorite club, using technical terms she didn't understand. I used our glasses and the salt and pepper shakers to position the defenders and the striker, and the cork from the bottle as a ball. As I was applying myself to this learned presentation, Léonard fell asleep. His head slowly came to rest on his arm, and he closed his eyes. He was exhausted after that penalty session that had forced him out of his comfort zone.

"I'll put him to bed."

I took my nephew in my arms and carried him to his room. I was surprised by how light he was. How old was he? Thirteen. If he continued with soccer, he'd have to do develop some muscles. I laid him in his bed and tucked him in.

Catherine had left the table and opened the little door that led from the kitchen into the backyard. Now she was leaning against the wall and smoking.

"He's already changed."

"Léonard, you mean?"

"Yes. It's obvious. Compared with that evaluation in the hospital. He's getting more confident. How many kids do you train?"

"It varies. Around twenty."

"They must love you."

"Oh, no, they're scared of me. I don't particularly like children, you know."

"You'll never make me believe that. You're a teacher."

"I used to be a player, but my knee gave up on me. When you've been kicking a ball since you were a teenager and you have to retrain, there aren't a whole lot of options."

"You could have coached adults."

"The job here attracted me. It just happened to be with young people."

She looked at me as she blew out smoke. There was a tinge of irony in her eyes. "Not easy to catch you out, is it?"

"I'm just giving you a straight answer."

"My friends liked you. They're a couple, by the way."

"I thought they were mother and daughter."

"The younger woman was one of my patients before she became a friend. Her mother was a manic-depressive. She lived in fear all through her childhood, but it was only when she grew up that she started having nightmares. She's much better now. She illustrates children's books. She draws monsters, but acceptable ones."

"You must see all kinds in your work."

"Pretty much."

It was early afternoon, and the neighborhood was totally quiet. The only sound was the birds in the gardens. We stood there for a moment without moving, in that corner of the yard, listening to them. Catherine was very close to my shoulder, and I was aware of it. It wouldn't have taken much for our skins to touch.

"Why did you choose a profession that's so . . . "

"So dark? You mustn't think that. There's also a lot of light. And besides, I needed to understand. I was, how can I put it . . . terrified, when I was small, by a feeling of absurdity. Understanding is my shield."

"And does it work?"

"It depends on what it's for. Shields protect you, but they also isolate you. Do you see what I mean?"

"Not really."

"I also have a sweat suit with holes in it."

"That must be the one thing we have in common."

"Do you think so?"

"I usually say what I think."

"You see me as a middle-class intellectual who goes to the theater after work."

"Isn't that true?"

"So what am I doing in this yard?"

"Taking an interest in a boy who suffers from Asperger's syndrome."

"I'm interested in people who are alone."

"Everyone's alone."

"Some people hide it less well than others. I feel more at ease with those people."

"You're going to burn yourself."

"I'm sorry?"

"With your cigarette."

21

When Léonard came out of his room, it was after eight. Catherine Vandrecken had left long before. I made pasta shells. He wanted to see more videos of penalties, but I refused. If he was starting to do sports regularly, he had to live a healthier life, especially when it came to sleep, and give up such an irregular rhythm. I could sense he didn't really agree, but he finished his food and went back to bed. I did the same soon afterwards. That day, like the previous ones, had worn me out.

When I woke the following morning, I thought about the leak under the kitchen sink. About my habits. About that discussion we'd had over lunch, Léonard, Catherine, and I. The reason I switched off the water every time I left the house was because of that damned leak. But why hadn't it occurred to me to repair it? Because I wasn't in my own home. What would Catherine Vandrecken have thought if I'd given that explanation for my behavior? Knowing her a little better now, I was sure that answer would have resulted in lots of deductions tinged with irony.

I made myself a coffee. The windowpanes were still covered with frost. Even after two days of sun, the ground was going to be brittle. I only had a few more days to put Léonard in a "real" match, to give him the feeling he'd actually gotten somewhere. An opportunity presented itself in the form of a friendly match before the under-16s championship, in which my team was supposed to meet the one from Valenciennes. But was it sensible to throw him into the lions' den on that occasion? In a training session, his moments of weakness were manageable. The group was less and less surprised by his reactions, and I still had the possibility of blowing the whistle for a break, to give him time to recover. In an official match, that would obviously be impossible. The problem wasn't his talent. The difference he could make with his approach to the game was quite real, I couldn't deny it, and he was even starting to open up to the others, but the fact remained that the sophisticated mechanism of his brain could stop at any moment, at the slightest grain of sand. How could I help him to make more progress? There had to be a method, there had to be exercises. I could talk about it with Catherine, but in such a short time, what did I hope to achieve? It was important to keep things simple and straightforward. That's what I thought. It was then that my gaze fell on the cabinet where the dishes and the flatware were kept. I remembered how much he now liked to lay the table, as evidence that he was mastering life in the house. An idea occurred to me. I was going to play a trick on him in my way, but in his interest. I changed knives and forks, glasses, bowls, plates, all the dishes, around in order to alter Léonard's points of reference.

I whistled as I took my shower. He'd be up soon, and I didn't want to miss his reaction to this little kitchen revolution. Deep down, I was pleased of getting my own back with this trick, after his listing of my habits in Catherine's presence. I even took the time to have a shave. In fact, by the time I left the bathroom, Léonard was already in the kitchen, not only that, he was having breakfast. I went to him, making an effort to conceal my surprise. He seemed quite calm, and nothing was missing on the table. Clearly, he'd found everything, and in record time. And the test didn't seem to have upset him in the slightest. I poured myself another cup of coffee and took a quick glance around. The drawers were in place, the closets tidy, no trace of a feverish search. I went back to the table and sat down opposite Léonard. He was eating his cereal with gusto, focused on his bowl. But after a short while, he deigned to make a comment.

"I know an exercise like that in chess. You ask the player to turn his back and you change all the positions. He has to find them again from memory and resume the game."

"But when Dr. Vandrecken took your seat, you were upset."

"That's not the same thing at all. That wasn't a game."

I didn't know what to reply. He started scraping the bottom of the bowl, as he usually did. With the end of his spoon, he was tracking down the smallest crumb.

"It's a really good test," he added. "But I think you need to add something extra."

"What's that?"

"An empty drawer."

"Why?"

"That's the most difficult thing for me, an empty drawer. I don't know what I'm supposed to do with it: leave it as it is, fill it, but then with what? Every time my mother moves, that's what scares me the most. All those empty spaces to fill."

22

For once, all the boys were there. Their parents must have thrown them out, tired of seeing them always lounging on the couch, glued to computer games, or else using up their phone contracts. I gathered them together in the middle of the field, making sure Léonard was some distance away. Coming out of the locker room, he had stayed at the back of the group, as usual, and as the boys moved into the the center circle, he'd continued toward his net, with his slightly strange way of moving, like a planet that didn't belong to the same solar system.

"We're going to have two short halves of twenty minutes each. I want intensity, and I want pace. Don't look for the knockout blow. Think about the match with Valenciennes. No hard tackles, okay?"

"Okay, sir!" they all said in unison.

I formed two groups, taking care to separate Cosmin and Léonard. I had an idea of the back of my mind and just before kick-off, while the boys were still warming up, I took Cosmin aside because he was the one I considered the best of my outfield players, the only one capable of grasping an instruction that was even slightly compex.

"I'd like you to approach this session in a different state of mind than usual," I said to him.

"Whatever you say, sir."

"I always ask you to respect the tactics I've laid out. You know why?"

"Of course. If you're not in the right place and don't prepare the play, you don't get anywhere."

"Except that if you always repeat the same tactics, your opponents remember them and find it easier to block them."

"That's also true, sir."

"So what I'm asking you today is to move out of your comfort zone."

"What do you mean, sir?"

He frowned. He knew perfectly well what I was talking about. But he was cautious by nature. He wanted to be sure he really understood how much free rein I was giving him.

"I mean I want you capable of going straight for the goal yourself, when everyone is expecting you to look for your center forward, or pass along the wings."

"Hogging the ball, sir. I thought you hated that."

"Well, today, that's what I'd like to see."

"Okay. You swear you won't kill me afterwards?"

"I swear."

I went back to the touchline. I heard the two sides calling each other names. They were excited by the dry, cold air, which made them want to get moving. I could happily have played with them. But I needed to keep my distance. Especially today, when I had that decision to make.

Léonard's team put pressure on the other team's goal, which was under siege for a good ten minutes. It never stopped, what with a bad save, a corner kick, the game never came back across the center circle, just kept returning to the other side, without Léonard having the slightest challenge to deal with. And then Marfaing blocked Bensaid, who'd become a bit isolated, and Cosmin took possession of the ball.

This was the moment I'd been waiting for. I looked to see where Léonard was, in his net. He seemed to have lost interest in the match. He was walking on his line, as if on a tightrope, looking down at his feet. I felt like crying out to alert him, but

I pulled myself together. It was much more interesting like this. For Cosmin's team, this was the ideal counterattack. Having put so much pressure on the goal, the other team had left their defense wide open and it was just a matter of finishing the job. Cosmin only had one last defender in front of him, Costes, who was trying to seem taller than he was by opening his arms wide. I wondered, at that moment, whether Cosmin was going to follow my instructions, or whether, conditioned by the previous training sessions, he was going to play it safe. In mid-run, he slowed down and saw Rouverand raising his arm. Of course it was the right thing to do. His center forward was absolutely alone, unmarked, the way he's shown on the blackboard in the locker rooms, and it would have been a mistake, a foul even, not to give him the ball.

Cosmin was no more than thirty yards from the goal. He prepared his move and Rouverand was already opening the inside of his foot to take his offering. But no. Cosmin continued running toward the goal. Costes had already moved, trying to block that imaginary pass to Rouverand. Cosmin ran into the penalty area and followed up with a cross that was perfection itself. He had indeed hogged the ball, run with it, and produced a beautiful piece of improvisation. But as I, and the boys on the field, watched wide-eyed, what happened next belonged to Léonard, and only to him. Just when it all seemed done and dusted, he got down on the ground full length and deflected the ball with his fingertips.

Where had he come from to make a save like that? How had he guessed the right side? The break, the feints, Cosmin's final play, everything had been too fast, and too well-executed, for the ball not to end up at the back of the net. Unless it met an exceptional goalkeeper on its way.

Cosmin ran back to his own team without making any bad-tempered gestures, incredulous rather, and the game resumed, but I could see from their faces that it was somehow over. If you couldn't beat Léonard with a move like that, nobody else had any chance of success, and his team was bound to score eventually. And that was what happened. Hervalet scored an own goal, as a sign of discouragement. What could you do against a Martian?

23

I walked with the boys to the locker room. That was something I didn't usually do, thinking that after a training session they'd already seen enough of me. But I had a premonition that something was going to happen, something bad. The day had been too perfect. Something was going to complicate everything. Life wasn't just that moment of grace when my nephew had lain down on the ball.

Some were already in the showers, others still recovering on the bench, but the atmosphere was strangely silent compared to the usual. Even Marfaing didn't make any of his terrible jokes. It was then that Rouverand yelled at Léonard. He spoke as if he represented the whole group and, in a way, it was true. He asked a question and I felt a flush of heat rise in me.

"Congratulations, Léo, on your save. But tell me something. Did you take a chance, or did you know he was going to put it there?"

It was now that things were going to turn nasty, of course. Changing the forks in a drawer, sitting on a couch watching videos: all that was just a game, just as Léonard himself had said. Quite the opposite of a locker room full of fourteen-year-old boys with raging hormones.

"Cosmin knows, he was in the front row, man!"

It was Marfaing who had spoken, and others said much the same. It was if everything held back so far was exploding. They all started talking at the same time, until Costes intervened.

"Hey, let's hear what he has to say!"

"Sorry, guys, but I can't answer. I put everything into my cross, that's all I can say. Léo's the one who knows."

This was it. They were all going to turn to him now, and the trap would close. He would give them one of those lectures he was so good at. They would hate him. And we'd have to start all over again from scratch.

"I took a chance."

"What?"

"A chance. That's your answer."

There was a moment of complete silence. Léonard's face was as inscrutable as ever, and everyone wondered for a moment if he wasn't playing a trick on them. Then there was a first burst of laughter, followed by another.

"Hell, Léo, if on top of that you're just lucky . . . "

"I don't agree," Bensaid said. "It was champion's luck."

"He's right!"

"In any case, it was great, man. Do the same for us against Valenciennes. That's all we ask!"

I waited for Léonard in the car. The locker room had given its verdict, but I was still postponing mine. My nephew joined me, and as soon as he closed the door I asked him the question that was on my mind.

"What you told Kevin, was that the truth?"

"No."

"So you lied?"

"Yes."

"I didn't think you ever lied."

"This time I had to."

"Why?"

Léonard gave a slight grimace, then started swaying gently in his seat. He must have made a considerable effort to overcome an invisible barrier inside himself. "I remembered that other time with him, when things went wrong."

I inserted the key in the ignition and started the engine. I couldn't help smiling. He'd constructed a new box.

"How did you know what Cosmin was going to do?"

"1973. AFC Ajax versus Bayern Munich. Johan Cruyff is in line with the goal, with two players backing him up. He feints to the left, then the right, and keeps the ball. The last feint to the right means that his cross goes to the left. That's the most frequent move."

"Frequent?"

"I don't have any example of a shot to the right when the last feint is to the right."

"What would you have thought if he'd shot to the right and beaten you?"

"I'd have added that variation to the others. But he didn't do that."

If he was capable of lying now, he was almost ready to live in society, so he might as well take part in an official match. When we left the parking lot, I turned right, not left as I usually did.

"Aren't we going home?"

"No. We have some shopping to do."

I drove onto the avenue that led to the center and parked close to the pedestrian zone. Léonard didn't ask me where we were going, as if he already knew I wasn't going to answer him. We crossed Place de l'Horloge and took the first street on the right. There it was. The last sports store in town that wasn't part of a chain. Gossin and Son. The only place that still sold hand-stitched boots.

"What are we doing here?" Léonard asked in front of the window.

"Getting some gear."

I went into the store, and Léonard followed me. I pointed him to the bench where the customers sat. A bald, thickset man of about forty came out from the back of the store. This was Gossin the son. He had a face like a bulldog, but when he recognized me, it lit up in a smile and he crushed my hand. Raymond had been a junior international, but had had to take over the family business when his father died unexpectedly. He always came to the stadium on match days, and without really talking much, we'd immediately liked each other.

"What can I do for you, Vincent?"

"This young man needs a pair of Zifrelis. And gloves. Do you still have your Buffons?"

"I don't get much opportunity to sell any, you know. A Stradivarius in Sedan, you know what I mean . . . But I'll see."

Léonard's face was inscrutable, as always. He waited, motionless, on the bench, looking at the posters of soccer legends that plastered the walls. Raymond came back, his arms loaded with boxes, but the first pair of boots was the right one. The Zifrelis fit snugly, while ensuring perfect stability. And it turned out there were still some Buffons. Léonard put them on and his hands stopped moving as if by magic. We left the store without saying anything to each other. It was the time when people were doing their shopping and the streets were crowded and noisy, with everyone in a hurry. Neither of us felt like walking quickly. Just before we got to the car, Léonard finally broke the silence.

"The boots I had were fine, you know."

"Fine for training, maybe. But for an official match, good gear makes all the difference."

He said nothing for a moment or two, as if unsure he had understood correctly. "Am I going to play in an official match?"

"Yes. Next Sunday."

We got back in the car. Léonard kept the boxes on his knees. "Thank you," he said.

"It isn't a gift, it's a loan. You'll pay me back when you sign your first contract."

"You really think I can become a good goalkeeper?"

"You already are."

"Does that cancel out your promise?"

"What promise?"

"You were supposed to learn chess. Do you remember?"

"It doesn't cancel out anything at all."

The traffic was heavy and it took us a good quarter of an hour to get out of town and reach the suburban area where my house was. I turned onto my street. There was a van in front of me moving slowly and, when it moved aside, I saw her, Madeleine. She was searching in the trunk of a garishly colored car, which she had parked right across the gate. She seemed very nervous. So she was the reason for my premonition. I'd gotten it wrong.

24

She had a new hairstyle, with bangs. She seemed even more nervous than the first time she'd come, but as if she'd read my thoughts, she made an effort to put on a big smile as if to say that she was in good shape.

Léonard was waiting on the sidewalk, holding back a little, and when Madeleine rushed to him and put her arms around him, he remained inert and looked away. My sister hugged him to her, kissed him several times, then, sensing that he didn't know what to do with this flood of affection, freed him from her embrace and turned back to me.

"You see, I kept my word, I'm even early!"

"Was your course shorter than expected?"

"No. I dropped out, and I'm not the only one. It was a scam."

"I thought the teachers were great."

"At first, but afterwards everything went wrong. I swear to you, it was crap, and besides, it's a race against time to open the bar by the beginning of November."

"The bar?"

"Patrice's bar in Rheims. You have no idea what's involved, especially as Patrice has left everything to me, he's taking care of raising the money, you understand, and finding sponsors. Without sponsors there's no point even opening, the clientele depends on word of mouth, the local bigwigs, the movers and shakers, that's the way it works!"

It was a real verbal Niagara. No way to stop her. She told me that she had to supervise the work, fight with the suppliers over the phone, deal with a thousand details a day. The way she told it, she was working 24–7.

"And with all this going on, what are you going to do about Léonard?"

"I admit I did wonder about that. I even thought to ask you for a bit of an extension. And then Patrice took things in hand, that's the way he is, you know, he's a man of action."

This Patrice was clearly a godsend. He'd managed to get an appointment at the best school in the region, and apparently it was possible to take in Léonard in the middle of the school year, except that the only day the principal of this sought-after establishment would agree to see them was tomorrow. Madeleine stopped to catch her breath. She looked at me for a moment. In spite of the effort I was making to hide my irritation, it must have been obvious.

"You don't seem pleased to see me. Is it because I arrived unexpectedly? I know you hate that, but it's in a good cause, I'm setting you free!"

There was another detail that had changed as far as her appearance was concerned. She was wearing high heels.

"I'm going inside, okay?"

I went into the house and Léonard walked past me and straight to his room. I remembered what Catherine Vandrecken had told me the first time we spoke. Children with Asperger's didn't have the same relationship to affection, to ties. They needed security and routine, but it wasn't linked to any person in particular. He could find all that in Rheims, and for a longer time. What did I have to give him that wasn't temporary? That's what I should have been thinking. The rest was misplaced sentimentality.

My sister now came into the house and headed straight for the kitchen. She'd found what she was looking for in the trunk of the car. It was a glass bottle containing a greenish liquid.

"I hope you don't mind, I'm going to eat my soup. It's all I eat, but I'm ravenous."

"Are you on a diet?"

"Have you noticed how fat poor people are? Poor people don't order champagne in trendy bars. Having a good figure in my work is really important. Did you see my bangs?"

"It makes you look different."

"It makes me look younger. That's Patrice's doing. He always says the secret of success is in the details."

She heated the soup in the microwave and poured it into a bowl. She sat down at the table to drink it, but it was too hot. Her high heels were hurting. She took her shoes off under the table. She started blowing on the surface of the liquid.

"Apart from that, anything to report about Léonard?"

"How do you mean?"

"I don't know, any problems you've had with him."

"No."

"Did you really manage to get him playing sports?"

"Yes."

The last thing I wanted was a discussion, let alone an argument. Anything that might make it obvious I was unhappy about his going.

"And he's been getting on okay?"

"Pretty well."

"You know, I really appreciate your help."

"I didn't exactly have any choice."

"I know what it cost you."

"Let's not exaggerate."

"And you must tell me what you spent on Léonard. You'll be repaid along with the rest."

"The rest?"

"The loan."

I looked at my sister. She put down the bowl. She realized we weren't on the same wavelength. She turned very pale. "You forgot."

"No. But I told you we'd talk about it face-to-face."

"You mean you can't do it."

"I didn't say that."

She launched into a sales pitch that included the fabulous prospects for the bar, Patrice's ability to generate money, like Jesus with the loaves, and even offered me a schedule of repayment with an 8-percent rate of interest. I made her out a check to stop her talking. I wanted them to leave quickly now.

Léonard came out of his room. He'd put his things in a plastic bag and was holding his chess set under his arm. He was ready. I walked them to the car. Léonard sat down in the passenger seat. My sister started the ignition. It was a pseudo-sports coupé, which compensated for its lack of power with lots of noise. I tried to imagine what Patrice looked like. There was something that didn't quite tally between the friend of bigwigs and the chromium-plated wheel rims of that car. I stayed on the sidewalk watching them drive off. The rear spoiler was loose.

I went back inside and locked the door. I tried to make myself coffee but there were no more cartridges. In Léonard's room, the two boxes from Gossin and Son lay on the chest of drawers. My nephew hadn't taken either the boots or the gloves with him. I sat down on the edge of the bed, as he often did, and looked through the window at nothing in particular. I'd been right not to change the wallpaper. Everything passed. You could never build anything.

25

I went back to my life the way it had been before Léonard. I left after nine for training without anybody waiting under the clock to put pressure on me. I'd never realized how silent the house was, apart from the leak under the sink, which could be heard more and more distinctly. As a safety measure, I replaced the bowl with a bucket.

I had a call from Catherine Vandrecken. When I saw her name, I didn't pick up but listened to the message. She asked after Léonard and suggested we meet this weekend. I was pleased to hear her voice, but I didn't call her back. I couldn't. I didn't see what we could say to each other, let alone do together, now. She left another message the next day, a very short one, asking me simply to call her back, then nothing else.

The day of the match against Valenciennes arrived. In the locker room, the boys were very nervous, as if they foresaw disaster. I'd told Favelic to go back to his old place in goal, but nobody was reassured by this decision, he least of all. None of the players mentioned Léonard as they put their shirts on, but everyone was thinking about him. They were going to miss the Martian, as Catherine had nicknamed him.

The match was a real disaster. Everything conspired to turn it into a humiliation. First of all, the guys from Valenciennes were pretty good, well-organized, realistic, while on our side, the team was like a building that had collapsed from the inside. The front held up for ten minutes, then everything fell down. Favelic communicated his restlessness to his defense, the midfield had to play very deep to compensate, which meant that the strikers didn't have enough ammunition. In other words, defeat was pre-programmed. I tried my best to shake them up at half time, but I didn't believe in it myself and they felt that. They conceded four goals and, frankly, there was still room for two more. The referee's final whistle came as a relief.

In the parking lot, the faces of the supporters and the few club members who'd braved the cold to come and watch this mess of a soccer game were unequivocal. They were worried. It was a friendly match of course, which didn't count for the championship, but the championship was starting in a few days and it was obvious that the team wasn't going to be transformed in such a short time. I saw the club's deputy chairman, Armand Vauquier, approaching. He'd come with his wife, and the poor woman was stamping her heels to warm herself, in a hurry to go.

"Not too good, was it, Barteau?" he said. "I hope things will be better for the match that counts!"

I could have reassured him. That was all he wanted. "Don't expect any miracles."

"Is it as bad as that?"

"What do you think? They're only average players."

"What do you mean by that?"

"That they don't have anything that makes them stand out."

He looked at me intrigued. Was it a criticism of the way the club was organized, its ability to attract young talents, or just words spoken in the heat of the moment by a somewhat depressed coach? He hesitated to sound me out any further, afraid maybe of where it might lead. His wife was signaling to him from a distance. He'd probably promised to take her to the Brasserie de l'Horloge, which served an excellent *choucroute*. He beat a retreat.

I saw my players in the locker room, but spared them the post-match pep talk. I knew perfectly well what I should have told them. Great teams didn't depend on one player. Nobody was to hide behind the loss of Léonard, and there was only one thing we could do, roll up our sleeves and work twice as hard. Except that I didn't believe in that argument. And neither did they.

When I got back home, I was immediately struck by a peculiar smell. The water had spread over the tiled floor of the kitchen and was starting to stagnate. The leak was clearly increasing, and a bucket wasn't enough to contain it anymore. I switched off the water at the meter, then grabbed a mop and a broom and made an effort to sweep the water out into the backyard. I had to do something about that leak, I knew. All I wanted was a respite. It was then that the doorbell rang. I was barefoot, in order to paddle in the water, and I had the broom in my hand. I opened the door. It was Catherine Vandrecken.

"I couldn't get hold of you. I was wondering if there was any problem."

She seemed not to notice either how I was dressed or the fact that I was clearly busy.

"No. Everything's fine."

"What about Léonard?"

"He's gone."

I could lie to my sister without any problem: she was so used to doing it herself that she'd lost any notion of a distinction between true and false. I could lie to myself up to a point. But I realized from the way Catherine was looking at me that it would be very difficult to lie to her. All the more reason to keep her at a distance.

"Aren't you going to ask me in?"

"No. I'm doing the housework, as you can see."

"I wanted to invite you to the theater."

"Don't do that."

"Why not?"

"You're wasting your time."

"That's not the impression I've had so far."

"Because Léonard was here."

"Do you think he was my only reason to see you?"

"What else?"

"You're angry."

"My boys lost this afternoon."

"Then maybe it's better if I come back another day?"

"If you like, but this won't be the only time they lose."

She realized she had a wall in front of her, but the more she tried to break through it, the more bricks and mortar I was going to put between us.

"See you later, then."

"Okay."

"You have my number."

I closed the door, taking good care to avoid Catherine's eyes. I stood there in the corridor for a moment, with that vision of her walking away into the darkness, then went back to the kitchen. I gave myself simple objectives: Make something to eat, don't go to bed too late. I opened the fridge and look for something that could be rustled up quickly, until I realized I couldn't do it. The mere idea of sitting in front of my plate, alone, in the harsh kitchen light, revolted me.

26

The only place in town where a bachelor could eat in peace was the station brasserie. When I first came to Sedan, I'd made it my canteen, then, when the regulars in the place had become a little too familiar to me, I'd preferred to stay at home, even if it meant just having pizzas delivered.

They'd changed the decor to attract a younger clientele, but apparently it hadn't worked. There were still the same two or three regulars propping up the bar, the card players, and that old woman who talked to herself, drank only dry white wine, and was constantly rummaging in her bag. I went straight to the back and sat down on a corner banquette. The manager had put in loudspeakers so that music could be heard in the farthest corners of the room, and had connected them to a radio station for teenagers. The place was like a nightclub waiting for customers. There was also a TV set placed high up on a wall, showing a 24-hour news channel with the sound off. Breaking news from all over the world, interspersed with commercials for insurance.

The waiter was also the same. A short, thin man with sparse hair. He nodded when he saw me, and spoke to me as if I'd been there the day before. He made an allusion to the match as he cleaned my table.

"So we lost, not a good start. The dish of the day is beef stew."

"That's fine."

"And to drink, a draft beer?"

"Yes."

I needed a beef stew. The kind of thing your grandmother made, though I'd never known mine. On my father's side, it was as if there had been nobody before him, though I'd finally figured out, overhearing a conversation between my parents, that there had been a big quarrel between my father and his father, although I never found out what it was about. On my mother's side, it was different, but the result was the same: She'd tell us about her mother with emotion in her voice and always promise us to go visit her, in the Vendée, except that the opportunity never arose and the old woman had died, remaining for us just a photograph on the sideboard in the living room. That family isolation had intrigued me, especially when I went to school. I saw my friends going on vacation to their grandparents' house, playing with their cousins, discovering other horizons, all those things that didn't exist for us. Why were we so isolated? Why didn't my parents have any friends? And then one day, I understood. New neighbors had moved in next door, and quite naturally they'd invited us over for drinks to get acquainted. My sister and I had gotten ready, quite excited because we knew they had children—possible friends—but suddenly we heard yelling in the house and realized, even before being told, that those drinks would never happen. My mother had burned my father's shirt in trying to iron it, the argument between them had become heated, and, in his anger, my father had given a chair in the living room an almighty kick and broken his foot. How could we ever have opened our door to neighbors, let alone cousins, when violence could break out at any moment in our house? From the window of my room, I saw my mother go next door to apologize, and we were told that if anybody in the neighborhood asked why my father was walking with crutches, we should say that he had fallen down the stairs.

The waiter came back with my beer and lingered to start a conversation. I'd forgotten that he was in the habit of doing that. He started by telling me in detail about his divorce and the lengths to which his ex-wife was going to take the little he owned away from him.

It was at that moment that I saw the blonde from accounting come into the brasserie. She had two men with her, and I heard her shrill laughter as they sat down at the bar.

"Nine and a half miles isn't bad, is it?"

The waiter was asking me a question, but I'd lost the thread. What was he talking about? Luckily, he didn't wait for my answer, but launched into a defense of running. The way he told it, it was running that had saved his life after his separation, and his goal now was to take part in the New York Marathon. He spoke about it with stars in his eyes. I was starting to feel hemmed in when the kitchen called him about my food, and he came back across the Atlantic, and again became, at least for the moment, a waiter in Sedan.

I thought I'd been saved, but it didn't last long. The girl from accounting was alone now at the bar. The guys she'd come in with had vanished as if by magic, and she was looking insistently in my direction. What was her name again? Béatrice. Our eyes met and she made a little sign to me, to which I had no choice but to respond. She came straight toward me, and as if that wasn't enough, the waiter, bringing my food, joined in.

"Shall I add another setting?" he asked with a knowing air.

What on earth had possessed me to leave home?

Béatrice was wearing an excessively open blouse and a very short skirt, but that was nothing compared with her make-up. There was something painful about her desire to seduce. She ordered the same thing as me and started eating and talking. She couldn't stop, as if silence scared her. The club, the town, the transportation, the weather, she had something to say about everything. And then she mentioned the two men she'd come in with, making it quite clear she hadn't been interested in them.

We avoided dessert, got as far as the coffee, and I thought I was over the worst, but it was then that she asked me if I could drive her home, because the neighborhood where she lived was rough. There are some evenings when nothing works for you. And so it was that this Béatrice found herself in my car, where she continued talking, on and on, panting as she did so. She lived in a small development on the edge of town, which seemed quiet enough, though it was true there wasn't a soul about at this hour, and not much light either. I walked her to the front door of her block. I thought about Meunier, for a brief moment. About his comment, "You're a strange guy."

She was getting ready to key in her code when she turned to me. In spite of her make-up, her would-be sexy outfit, and the mountain of words she'd erected between us, I found the expression on her face at that moment quite touching. She looked so lost. Why couldn't I simply have a good time with her? Do her some good, and me too? Because Catherine Vandrecken had knocked at my door? But Catherine was an idea, a utopia, like Mila, years earlier. The reality was girls like Béatrice, matches against Valenciennes, Léonards who left as they had come, problems with the plumbing. It was high time I realized it. There was no magic, or else it was temporary, and believing in that illusion was dangerous. Because after a while the show ended, the lights came back on, and you felt like a fool. And that's why I found myself in Béatrice's apartment. As if I wanted to put even more distance between the emotions I'd felt over the past few days and my possible life.

It was a tiny place, and even more alarming in that she'd painted the walls bright red. I sat down on the black imitation-leather couch, which probably unfolded to become her bed, and she offered me a glass of whiskey, then slipped away into the bathroom.

I downed my whiskey in one go and poured myself another glass. A painting, or rather a lithograph, was hanging on the opposite wall. It showed a white-faced clown, shedding tears the color of blood. I looked around for a stereo, but couldn't see one, so I sat down again and waited, facing the clown. Béatrice was still in the bathroom. She must have been in there for about fifteen minutes and I was starting to get worried. I went to the door and heard sobs. She was crying without stopping, as if her whole being had been released. What could I do? I hesitated, then made up my mind to open the door cautiously. It was then that she sprang out like a jack in the box and started hitting me with all her might. When I tried to hold her back, she began biting and scratching me and screaming.

"All you want is to fuck me! What do you take me for? A hooker? I'm not a hooker!"

I tried to parry that avalanche of blows. Her strength was increased tenfold by her anger. It was really scary. She grabbed hold of a vase and threw it in my direction. It narrowly missed me and literally exploded against the wall.

"Out! Get out, you bastard!"

The door was just behind me, and I only had to reach out my hand to open it. Béatrice gave me a last kick before locking herself in. She kept yelling, threatening to call the police, to bring charges, to drag me into court if I kept harassing her.

I stood for a while in the corridor, motionless, trying to recover. A neighbor came out of his apartment, three doors down. He was a man of about fifty, in his pajamas. He didn't seem surprised to see me there. He shrugged.

"You got off easy. She ran after the last one with a knife."

27

Entering the house, I was immediately aware of something abnormal. A muted moaning sound in the darkness. It took me a moment to realize it was the pipes.
For some reason, cutting off the water had set off terrible vibrations that spread through the walls. I went down into the basement. I just had to switch the water back on for the vibrations
to stop, but in that case, I'd have to get up every two hours to
empty the bucket. I preferred to leave the valve closed.

I retreated to my room. I'd had enough for today. Except
that the vibrations in the pipes followed me there. And it was
like that throughout the house. Only the two rooms at the back
were spared. I tried to settle in the larger one, but I'd forgotten how smashed in the bed was, and so I fell back on the one
Léonard had occupied. I really did try to sleep then. But everything was against me. The size of the bed, which forced me to
lie across it. That horrible wallpaper, whose image persisted
well after I'd closed my eyes. The scratches from that poor girl,
which I wasn't in any mood to treat. I was like a diver who
wants to go as deep as possible but keeps coming back to the
surface. After several attempts, I gave up. Best to turn on the
light, which is what I did.

I sat up with my back against the wall and pondered in the
silence. I remembered Catherine walking away without turn-
ing around after I'd rejected her so brusquely. I had the idea of
writing her a message to apologize, but I feared the consequences. I'd done the hard part, why go back? Why leave my

door open? It led nowhere. It was then that I noticed the exercise book on the windowsill. I stood up and leafed through it. It was the one that Léonard had used to write down soccer tactics, after his precious notes on chess. Had he left it deliberately, or had he forgotten it? After skimming through it at random, I started reading it more carefully, from the beginning.

As an introduction, Léonard had written some basic thoughts about chess, so obvious and so clear that even I could understand them, then in the following pages, he suggested some elementary combinations with which to start a game. I read these recommendations, all accompanied by sketches, with the greatest attention. It wasn't so abstract after all, not when explained by a clear-sighted player. Then I remembered the promise I'd made my nephew during the penalty session: to learn this game that seemed so distant from me, from the things I knew, as a response to the challenge he had set himself. I plunged back into reading the exercise book. I forgot the leak. The Valenciennes match. That moment of madness in Béatrice's apartment. I even forgot about Catherine Vandrecken, and by the time I got to the end of the book, I realized that dawn was breaking. The tension in me had subsided. I fell asleep.

28

B y the time I woke, it was quite late and I had three messages from Meunier on my phone. He didn't understand why my players were training on their own.

I jumped in my car and drove to the stadium on autopilot. Meunier was leaning on the railing, talking on the phone. When he saw me, he hung up. I could have sworn the conversation had been about me.

"What's going on with you? I was starting to get worried." He came a little closer to get a look at my cheek. "What's that? Have you been fighting?"

Béatrice's attack had left its mark on me.

"It's nothing. Did you start them running?"

"Sure."

"You did the right thing."

I walked away, intending to go onto the field and join the boys.

"Wait!" Meunier said behind me.

I stopped and sighed. One of Meunier's functions was to pass on messages from the club's management. I had a feeling I already knew what this one was about.

"There's something we need to talk about."

"Can't it wait?"

"It's important, Vincent."

At that moment my phone rang.

"Monsieur Barteau? This is the teaching hospital in Amiens South. I'm calling about your mother. Gabrielle Barteau."

My first thought was that she'd died. I stood there with my mouth open. The boys were starting a new lap and Meunier was watching me.

"She has to give up her room today," the voice on the phone continued.

"I don't know anything about that."

"Actually, we've been trying to reach your sister, Madeleine Barteau, who was due to come and fetch her. But we haven't heard from her. And since your name is also on the list . . . "

"What list?"

"Of people to contact."

Madeleine had given them my number without asking me. This was getting better and better.

"I can give you the number she left me. It isn't hers, but they pass messages on."

"Can't you call her yourself? We're very busy here, you know. And besides your mother is taking up a room we need."

"What will happen if nobody comes for her?"

"We're entitled to call an ambulance and have her taken home."

"Then do it."

"Monsieur Barteau, your mother is at the end of her life. She needs 24-hour care, and as I'm sure you understand, it's up to the family to face up to its responsibilities."

I tried to catch my breath, as if I'd been elbowed by an opposing defender just as I was about to receive a corner kick.

"I'll contact my sister, I'm sure there's been some misunderstanding."

"Your mother's leaving day was scheduled a long time ago."

"I told you I'll contact my sister."

"We really can't keep her, you know."

"Leave me a number and I'll call you back."

Immediately I'd hung up, I started going through the numbers. Madeleine had better answer me, and quickly.

"Sorry to say this, Vincent, but you've been a bit strange for a while. And I'm not the only one to have noticed."

I looked up. I'd almost forgotten he was there. Meunier. "What do you mean?"

"The deputy chairman didn't much like the way you answered him after the match against Valenciennes."

"Oh, yes? Would he have preferred it if I'd told him lies?"

"He'd have preferred it if you were pleased with the effort we make for young people in this club by giving them, a professional coach, who's quite well paid, by the way."

"Ah, so that's it."

"And apart from that, I don't see your little prodigy anymore."

"First of all, he's not my prodigy. He's just my nephew, and he's gone away with his mother."

"That's a bit stupid, isn't it?"

"Nobody ever said he would stay. Can I go back to my boys now?"

"You need to be more careful, though."

"About what?"

"I don't know. You're really not looking well."

Maybe he was right. Maybe the one thing I wanted was to chuck it all in. I looked him in the face and gave him a smile, then left him standing there, in his pearl gray suit.

Since I'd been in charge of the under-16s, I'd never missed a training session, and I'd never been late. I thought they were going to tease me, but they didn't. There were no comments, no nasty looks. They got down to the practice exercises I set them, as if everything was normal, they even seemed to apply themselves more than usual, and when the time came for the customary short match, Marfaing came up to me on behalf of the whole group.

"Don't worry about us, sir. We can do our two thirty-minute

halves. If you have something to sort out, we can carry on with-out you."

For them to react like that, it must have been really obvious that I was worried. I placed myself behind the goal and called Madeleine on the three numbers she'd used lately. Her room-mate hadn't heard from her and was clearly waiting with some impatience for her to settle two late rent payments. The class-mate she'd borrowed a phone from barely remembered her. The third number was Patrice's. It was permanently engaged, but I didn't give up and eventually managed to leave a mes-sage.

29

When I left the stadium, I had a vision of my almost empty fridge, and I immediately set off for the supermarket. There was no way I'd go back to the brasserie. I walked along the aisles, pushing the cart in front of me, staring straight ahead. I hardly knew what I was buying. I was on auto-pilot. I'd come level with the product and my hand would grab the pack and throw it in the cart before I'd had time to think. It was then that my phone vibrated.

"Vincent?" It was Madeleine.

I felt like yelling at her, but I stood there with the cell phone in my hand for a few seconds to calm down. "What's this nonsense about our mother?"

"I swear they gave me another date for her coming out. They really are idiots!"

"You'd better call them as soon as you can and then go straight there, or they're going to throw her out on the street."

"What? There's no way I can move from here. Not for two days at least! I'm alone with all the building work, and Patrice is in Germany negotiating with a brewery."

"You deal with it, I don't want to know."

"Vincent—"

"No."

"Vincent, at least listen to me—"

I hung up. The cart was almost full. I had enough to withstand a siege, which was what I was planning to do. I'd been had once, I wouldn't be had again. I went through the check-out and crossed the parking lot to my car. I was loading my purchases in the trunk when my phone rang again.

"Give me two days, Vincent," Madeleine resumed. "Please. Two days to find a solution, and then I'll leave you alone forever, you'll never hear from me again. Two days, Vincent. Nobody can take my place. If there's a problem on-site, we lose everything!"

I kept quiet. She must have been wondering if I'd hung up. She started crying.

"No, not that. Stop it right now."

I sat down on the edge of the trunk. I mustn't forget what had happened with Léonard. How my sister, all because she was in trouble, had managed to screw things up for me.

"Have you contacted anyone to take care of her after she leaves the hospital?

"Yes. A woman who's already taking care of her a little bit, and who seems nice. But I need to meet her to make the final arrangements. It can't be done long-distance. It was planned for another date."

"Give me her number."

"She'll tell you what she told me."

I paused to catch my breath. I closed my eyes. I couldn't get over what I was about to say. "Give me the number. I'm going there."

"Vincent, I—"

"Listen to me. I'm going to get her out of the hospital, take her home, and come to an arrangement with the caregiver. And that's it. You come there, and then I'm out of it."

"You know, I—"

"Give me the fucking number."

Once she'd given me the contact details for someone named Madame Robin, I hung up. I stood there in the parking lot, behind the car, the cart beside me. It was as if I was watching my own life unfold in front of me like a play. I was going to see Saint-Quentin again. All those years to get away from it, and I was going back. That barrier I had built, strengthened, every day, every hour, stubbornly, hadn't been enough. In the end, I was only two hours' drive from my childhood. What an idiot I was.

30

I set off without anything in my stomach. The sooner this business was settled, the better. It started raining before Amiens and I lost my way. I must have gone at least twelve miles too far. The town had changed a lot. I stopped in a service station and had a sandwich that had no taste. I finally spotted some signs pointing to the teaching hospital. It was a real treasure hunt, but just before two in the afternoon I drew up in the parking lot of the hospital.

At reception, I was pointed in the direction of the office, where I had to answer questions I had no answer for. My mother's medical record was a mess; she owed lots of money to the hospital, and nothing had been done according to the rules. Then I was told how to get to the oncology department, because before I could collect my mother, I had to speak with Professor Charlier, who had operated on her several times. I sat down in a waiting room with people who'd been through chemo. Opposite me, a five-year-old boy with a shaved head was doing a jigsaw puzzle.

Professor Charlier saw me in his office. I was surprised by how cramped it was. He looked tired and overworked, but his eyes were piercing.

"Are you the son?"

He started by running through my mother's medical history. He spoke concisely, without beating around the bush, and without taking refuge behind complex language. From the breast to the pancreas, the cancer had spread throughout her body over the years and become generalized. The professor had negotiated a few truces with the disease, but never gained a real victory. And now he was laying down his arms.

"Another operation would be pointless. These days, society has realized that it's more humane for the terminally ill to be with their families rather than in hospital."

I understood what he was saying, but wondered if there was anything humane about my return to Saint-Quentin. I struck me more as high-risk. I found myself in an elevator, holding the case history of Gabrielle Barteau, née Lemoine. I quickly looked through it and closed it again. I knew the ending.

The floor was reserved for terminal patients. I got a better idea of why the hospital was in such a hurry to retrieve any bed they could. It was like a military hospital struggling to cope with the ferocity of the fighting. Stretchers blocked the corridor, cables hung from the ceiling, the staff seemed in a constant hurry. Suddenly I saw my mother. They had already taken her out of her room so that a nurses' aide could disinfect it. She was waiting in a wheelchair, a blanket over her shoulders. She was wearing a wig, and the skin stretched across her face seemed to pull her jaw back, forcing her to keep her mouth open all the time. I came level with her and she looked at me with her little black eyes. She didn't show any surprise, let alone any emotion. She must have been warned, but that wasn't the main reason for her attitude. She seemed to have come back from a long way away, from a country you can't talk about to those who haven't been there, a country that changes your perception of the present and considerably reduces its importance.

"I'm thirsty," she said.

There was no breath in her voice, but in spite of everything, it was audible, as long as there wasn't too much noise around. A nurse arrived.

"Where can I get some water?"

"At the end of the corridor, on the right. You can keep the wheelchair to take your mother down, but you'll have to leave it at reception. You can hire another one, if you want to."

I pushed my mother to the elevators. Being behind her suited me perfectly. It helped me get used to her. I could see the pins keeping the wig in place over her real, sparse hair. Her blemished hands. She drank from a paper cup at the water cooler, almost greedily.

We crossed the lobby. The sun was low in the sky. I took hold of her emaciated body and placed it in the back seat. I gave up the wheelchair and hired another, since I had no choice. I had to struggle to fold it and fit it in the trunk. I thought I'd never manage. I sat down at the wheel, feeling that I'd gotten through the first stage. The hardest part was still to come. Saint-Quentin. I'd sworn never to set foot there again. But there it was.

As soon as the car set off, my mother fell asleep. Before handing her over to me, the nurse had given her some tablets, two in one go, and had left me what remained in the box, advising me to use them sparingly. "She'll sleep for a while now," she said, adding, "Old people don't like being moved."

31

Entering Saint-Quentin, I found that the town hadn't changed as much as all that, at least in the center, but when I got to the neighborhood where I'd spent my childhood, I revised my judgement. The little houses had almost all been torn down to make way for apartment blocks. A supermarket had replaced the movie theater, and the park had become a parking lot. I turned onto Rue des Cordiers. I had the impression it had shrunk, like my mother, and I almost missed the house. I had to back up to come level with it. How low and gray it was. Nobody had lived in it for a long time. Or maybe just ghosts.

I searched in my mother's bag for the keys. It was a complete mess in there. I thought I was going to have to wake her. Had she entrusted them to a neighbor? And then I came across them. They were in a separate pocket, along with a photograph of Léonard, her grandson. It was a poor-quality snapshot. He must have been three or four. His head already had that unusual shape, and his arms almost touched his knees. I quickly put it back and opened the door of the house.

The smell caught me by the throat. So it was still there after all these years, that horrible sewer stench. My parents had endlessly called in professionals, had work done, the drains changed, but without any improvement. It was still a joke. I tried to concentrate on simple thoughts. I just had to settle my mother at home and leave again. I went to the room that had been my parents'. The mantelpiece was sagging from the weight

of the ornaments and framed photographs. A pair of slippers
lay on the carpet.

I went to fetch my mother from the car. The back of her
neck was resting on the top of the seat and she was breathing
hard, with her eyes closed. I slid my hand between her back
and the seat and lifted her without her waking up. I put her
down on her bed, fully dressed, and covered her with a blanket, the first one I found. This was stage two, and the fact that
she was knocked out with sedatives suited me just fine. Now I
had to settle the question of the caregiver. I dialed her number
to tell her I'd arrived at the house, which was what we'd agreed
when I called her earlier in the day. But just as I was starting to
relax, she told me she couldn't be there for an hour because of
another lady she was looking after who had fallen downstairs.

A whole hour, waiting in this house. What the hell could I
possibly do? I thought to call Madeleine again, but what would
have been the point? To tell her I had the situation under control? To reassure her? Definitely not. To calm my nerves?
Forget it. I picked up the bunch of keys again and opened the
back door of the house. I felt my throat tighten. Nothing had
changed, or almost nothing, although, of course, the garden
was a bit overgrown. The flagstones, the scrawny rectangular
lawn with a stone wall on one side and a hedge on the other,
the cherry tree smack in the middle, the hut at the far end with
an open shed next to it that served as a storeroom for tools,
household products, anything that couldn't be kept in the
basement. Everything was the same. It was in this garden that
the battle with my father had reached its height. Since I wasn't
allowed to go out, or have friends, I'd spend most of my time
here, running and kicking a ball. I had a route that I repeated
to the point of exhaustion. I'd start from the flagstones, with
the ball at my feet. The wall was an imaginary teammate and
I'd pass the ball to him. He'd return it with a greater or lesser
degree of precision, depending on how the ball hit the stone.

I'd dribble past the cherry tree and find myself in a position to shoot, facing the shed, which represented the goal and in front of which I'd placed the mower as a goalkeeper you really couldn't get past. I indulged in this exercise so often that I became quite skilled, so skilled that I ended up knowing every stone in the wall off which the ball bounced and could pass to myself on the other side of the cherry tree and attempt a volley as I ran. In this way, I could sometimes put the ball away in the top corner—in other words, the corner of the shed—five or six times in a row. But of course I sometimes got carried away a little and my ball went too far and caused damage in the shed, which I'd then try to repair, without quite succeeding. One day, I even broke a pane of glass in the shed in a slightly too optimistic attempt at a lob. And when my father came home, I was given one of the most memorable beatings of our whole shared history, to the point where I pissed in my pants. In his eyes, I saw a desire to kill me, and he might have done it if I hadn't answered him back, saying, "Go on, get it over and done with." That stopped him in his tracks. As far as he was concerned, I'd once again tried to provoke him, and that's what had driven him crazy. He just couldn't conceive of the fact that a child needed to let off steam, that in being prevented from leaving the house he'd end up hitting the walls.

I opened the door of the hut. It didn't resist much. I had to bend a little to get inside. Here too, everything was in its place, even though dust covered the work bench, the pigeonholes, the wood stove, which my father lit in winter, at a time when he spent his weekends doing DIY projects. I wondered if the miniature garage was still there. I stooped to look under the work bench. There it was. I pulled it out from a pile of planks and put it down in front of me, blew on it, gazed at it. All that was missing was the ramp that had allowed the cars to park on the upper level, but the structure still held. I'd spent hours playing with that garage. My father had made it for me when

I'd caught pneumonia in the schoolyard one very cold winter and had stayed home for several weeks in the middle of the school year, recovering.

That was the kind of man he'd been, too. Sometimes I forgot it. But that was before he'd gone downhill. Before he went, in a few years, from being an indispensable foreman, proud of the trailers his workshop produced, to a traveling salesman, ripping off the innocent, and especially the poor, luring them with the virtues of buying on credit, until he again ended up unemployed. Maybe that explained why I was so mistrustful of the human race: the way my own father had changed, a transformation I'd lived though in real time during my childhood. If he'd been a violent person from the start, I think I could have accepted it, thought I'd been unlucky with the circumstances of my birth, and that was all. But this was different. I was present when the sickness started. I saw how easily madness could take hold of a man who built wooden garages, took you on his lap, read you stories. I watched my father become, almost in spite of himself, a wild animal whose only wish was to break me, lock me up, because he'd lost his job. Because society had destroyed him. If we were at the bottom of the heap, it meant you couldn't trust anyone. Nobody was safe from degradation, and that included me. It all depended on circumstances. That meant you needed a referee and red cards, and always to stay on the alert.

32

I wondered if the caregiver would ever show up. The hour had long passed. And then I heard her parking her car, a door slamming. Through the kitchen window, I saw a short, round, redheaded woman, limping a little and carrying a shopping bag. No sooner did I open than she was already in the corridor. She was used to the house. I held out my hand, but she took my arm and kissed me.

"She's told me so much about you," she said, "I have the feeling I know you. Is she asleep?"

"Yes."

"They must have given her Nordax. That'd knock a horse out. There's a problem, Vincent. I prefer to tell you right away."

She emptied the contents of her bag onto the kitchen table. There were cloths and things for washing. Then she turned to face me. She had eyes of amazing clarity.

"When your sister suggested I look after your mother part-time, I didn't say no, but now . . . I have this other lady I look after who's just fallen downstairs, and she's going to need me full-time. That's why I'm late. We had to talk and change the contract. I had to reassure her. She's no barrel of laughs, I can tell you, I'd much have preferred your mother, believe me!"

We were in the middle of the little kitchen. I didn't remember the place being quite so dark. I wasn't sure I quite understood. "What are you trying to tell me?"

"Oh, I won't leave you in the lurch, Vincent, I'll find you someone."

"You can't stay?"

"No. I just explained."

I retreated to the stone sink. I needed something to lean on. "Did Madeleine know you were looking after someone else?"

"Of course."

"You told her you'd only be part-time?"

"Obviously."

"Because we need someone full-time."

"Oh, I didn't realize that."

"When exactly did you speak to her on the phone?"

"Your sister? Well . . . Would you like a coffee? I could do with one. Don't worry, I know where it is."

I was in the house in Saint-Quentin, with my mother, and things were getting complicated.

"It's strange to see you in the flesh, you know. Her idol!"

"You must have the wrong son."

"April 17."

"What about April 17?"

"That's your birthday."

"Yes, I know that, thanks."

"Every April 17, she cries. And when she says, 'my big boy,' well, that says it all."

"Madame Robin—"

"Christiane, please."

I paused to catch my breath. I had to stop myself from drowning. "Christiane, could you at least look after her for, let's say, ten days?"

"No, I really—"

"Just until my sister gets here."

"I'm sorry, but it's not possible... Contracts are no joke. You can lose your license. As I told you, this other lady's a tough cookie, and if I—"

At that moment, a muffled noise was heard, coming from the bedroom. We both rushed there. My mother had fallen, probably trying to go to the toilet. She had thrown up all over herself. Her cardigan, her blouse, her skirt, it was everywhere.

"Well, that's very nice, isn't it?" Christiane Robin said.

We had to undress her, and wash her in the bath. She couldn't stand and I kept her upright as best I could, while Christiane rinsed her down with the shower.

"I'm going to find her some things. I know where they are."

I found myself drying her. She was trying to pull herself together. Her eyes were closed and she was struggling to open them.

"I'm sorry," she said.

"Try to hold on to the edge of the bath."

She gripped it with her hand, and it was only now, as I dabbed her skin with the towel, that I saw the scars from her operations. Her chest had been butchered, her abdomen opened from one side to the other.

Christiane came back with clothes, everything she could find that was warm and comfortable. We swaddled her—that's the only word I can find for it—then took her to the bed, each supporting her under one arm.

"It's better when you've thrown up, isn't it, Gaby?" Christiane said.

My mother replied by lifting her hand a little, but didn't open her eyes. She fell asleep again immediately. The trip to the bathroom had exhausted her.

The coffee was cold and I reheated it. I poured a cup for Christiane, but didn't have one myself. I was already too nervous.

"The worst of it is that pain is the only thing she has now. It's sad to say, but that's how it is."

"You know her local doctor?"

"Don't talk to me about him. A real son of a bitch. Pardon my language, but that's what he is. He's a Catholic, a real one, a fundamentalist like Monseigneur What's-his-name, the one who says that abortion is murder."

"I don't see the connection—"

"Because as far as he's concerned, pain is part of redemption, and so he never gives morphine. I know because he took care of my niece and she had a hard time of it to the end, but it was so that her sins could be forgiven."

"There are other doctors, aren't there?"

"You obviously don't know how things work around here. They don't take each other's patients in a town like Saint-Quentin, it's too small."

"And the hospital?

"It's not their problem anymore when it happens outside. They can't even cope with what happens inside! What you need in a case like this is to know people, otherwise . . . Vincent, I have to go. You're going to hate me but these are my working hours right now. I'll come back later if you want me to."

She kissed me again. I was starting to get used to it. She looked me in the eyes as she held my arm. She squeezed it tight. I never knew a woman could have such a strong grip. "It's good that you've come," she said. "Things will be better for her now."

I sat down on a kitchen chair. I heard her drive away. She was exactly the person my mother needed. But she wasn't free. I glanced around me at this room where my mother would take shelter with her sponges and her scrub brush when my father's madness made the walls shake. I had often hoped they'd both die. That they'd be laid forever under the ground, forgotten. But I hadn't foreseen the pain, I hadn't foreseen the scars.

I washed the cups mechanically. The cold water on my hands did me good. I'd often stood on a stool and floated wooden boats in that sink. That was a thousand years ago, or maybe yesterday. And then I thought again about what Christiane Robin had said, that you needed to know people when you were in this kind of situation. I saw Catherine's lovely face outside my door, the evening she came to ask me if everything was all right. I did know people. I looked for Dr. Vandrecken's number. I was quite capable of having deleted it. No, I still had it. I called, thinking she was seeing patients, getting ready to leave a message. But it was her voice I heard, as close as if she was in the room.

"Vincent?"

"I need you, Catherine."

33

C hristiane came back just before eight. I informed her of my decision to take my mother away. As far as she was concerned, it had been obvious from the start. She packed her bag, while I made up a kind of bed in the back of the Peugeot. When everything was ready, we gave my mother one more tablet and took her out in the blanket. Her size made the operation easy, and we were able to stabilize her on the seat. Christiane kissed Gabrielle on the forehead, then me, too, and wished me a safe journey.

At that time of day and that season, the road between Saint-Quentin and Sedan wasn't very busy. I hardly needed to use the brakes. At one point, my mother spoke in a language that was part of her dream.

There was a free parking space just outside my house. I was able to open the door of the house and come back to get my mother without any difficulty. I put her in the big room at the back, the one that Meunier had lived in for a few months. I brought water. I made sure the bedside lamp was working. My mother was still breathing, her mouth open, slightly obscenely. I put my hand on her forehead. It wasn't a caress, I wanted to see if she had a temperature. Her arm was hanging a little and I placed it by her side. I left the room.

Catherine arrived soon afterwards. She was wearing a sweater with a very high turtleneck and her hair was pulled back. She passed me, went to the table, and put down what she'd been able to obtain from Dr. Mérieux. The morphine and the syringes.

"Do you know how to give an injection?"

"Yes."

She closed her bag again, gave me a discreet smile, and headed for the door.

"What are you doing?"

"You asked me for help. There it is."

"Stay."

"I'm not the kind of person who throws herself at people, you know."

I caught her by the arm. "Catherine, forgive me. You scared me."

"Me?"

"Yes. You're too intelligent, too . . . I didn't feel as if I was in my place."

"What place?"

"Please stay."

There was a fiery look in her eyes. That was something I hadn't seen in her before. And then she softened. "You must be exhausted."

A moan came from the corridor. The effect of the Nordax was wearing off. Catherine went with me to the bedroom. My mother was gripping the sheet. It was as if she was trying not to slide off, which would have been very painful. We moved her back to the middle of the bed. Catherine lifted the sleeve of her nightdress. Her arm was as thin as a twig. Catherine looked for the vein, put the syringe in, and the liquid spread through my mother's body.

"Have you eaten?" Catherine asked me.

"No, but I'm okay."

"I'll make you something. Stay with her."

Catherine left the room. Soon afterwards, my mother gave a little chuckle, and almost immediately her eyes opened. "Vincent."

"Yes."

"I don't know this room."

"You're in my house. In Sedan."

She smiled and was silent for a long time. It was as if her whole body was relaxing. Then she tensed again slightly. "Your sister. Have you heard from her?"

"She's in Rheims. She couldn't come because she's working."

"And Léonard?"

"He's with her."

"That boy's a wonder."

"I know."

"Have you met him?"

"He came here."

"His father . . . his father thought he was crazy. He was ashamed of him. That's why he left Madeleine. She always ends up with men who . . . She's unlucky that way. I'd so much like to see the boy before I die. To hold his hand . . . Do you think he'll come?"

"Of course."

"I'd be so pleased . . . "

She sighed and closed her eyes. I assumed she wanted to speak some more. Her mouth made as if to utter a word, but she fell asleep again, and this time I turned out the light.

Catherine was making ham and eggs. She seemed quite at home in that kitchen. She'd half opened the window, to let out the smoke from her cooking and her cigarette.

"How is she?"

"She smiled. She even spoke to me, and then she fell asleep again."

"It's the morphine. I made do with what I could find. Do you have any wine?"

"I think so."

"I could really do with a glass."

I laid my hand on a bottle of Irancy. I always had a bottle or two, in case I had guests, except that I never did. Luckily, it wasn't corked. Catherine drank her wine, with her back to the counter, while I ate with gusto. I was on the last mouthful when my phone vibrated. An unknown number: It was Madeleine. I went out into the backyard.

"It's your sister. I'm calling you from the bar. I was worried when I didn't hear from you. How's it going?"

"Ma's at my house."

There was a silence on the line.

"What's going on, Vincent?"

"What's going on is that Madame Robin isn't free and her doctor's an idiot. What's going on is that I didn't have any choice. That seems to be the fashion right now."

"But you can't keep her."

"Keep her? Madeleine, you don't seem to understand. She's dying."

"Ma? She's as strong as a rock. She already pulled that one on me twice."

"I don't think there's going to be a third time. She wants to see Léonard."

"I told you, Vincent, I'm stuck here."

"I'm not asking you to bring him. I can come there and fetch him."

There was a second silence. "That won't be possible."

"I'm sorry?"

I could hear her breathing. At least ten seconds went by before she replied.

"He's in a specialist institution. He can't come out."

She couldn't have done that. I wanted to believe I was wrong. "You mean that highly regarded school?"

"No. That didn't work out."

"Do you mind explaining?"

"He threw a fit in his first class. You know, those few days with you . . . " "What of them?"

"Well, he's been a bit strange since then. He's withdrawn,

nobody can get close to him. In the apartment, he started breaking things. An apartment we'd been lent temporarily! I went to
see a specialist."

"A specialist in what?"

"Difficult children. He recommended an institution. He
may have . . . some kind of schizophrenia."

"What he has is nothing like that!"

"How do you know?"

"Madeleine . . . "

I felt like throwing it all in her face, her denial, her cow-
ardice, her lack of awareness, but at the last moment I
restrained myself. I knew my sister well enough to know that
driving her into a corner at a time like this would only make
matters worse.

"Vincent, are you still there?"

"Yes."

"I'll see what I can do about Léonard. I'll call you back.
And as soon as I can get away to see Ma, I'll be there."

"If you say so."

"Are you angry with me?"

I hung up. I didn't go straight back into the house. I was
hoping that the tension throughout my body would subside.
Catherine came out and joined me. She had a glass for me too.

"I don't drink."

"You don't drink, you don't smoke."

"I'm a sportsman."

"Try, just for this evening."

Reluctantly, I took the glass. I felt the liquid run down my
throat. I had to admit that, at that moment, it was exactly what
I needed.

"Léonard is in a special home. A shrink told my sister he's
schizophrenic."

Catherine turned pale. "It seems to me you need to take a
trip to Rheims."

"I'm thinking the same. But what do I do with my mother?"

"I could stay."

"I can't ask you to do that."

"Of course you can. I've always dreamed of having a mother to look after."

34

I left for Rheims before day had even risen. My plan was to arrive unexpectedly before Madeleine had time to put up any smokescreens. I knew where to go. The bar. She'd told me that its location would make it *the* place to be for every party animal in town. It was situated on a square behind the cathedral, opposite the movie theaters. It should be easy enough to find.

I drove into the town just before ten in the morning and headed for the historic center. I saw the cathedral looming up in front of me, and drove around it. It was market day, and I realized I needed to park quickly. I continued on foot and came to the square with the movie theaters without even searching. The bar was on the other side. From a distance, you could see scaffolding. The front of the building was being renovated.

As I approached, I saw that the double door was open because of the smell of paint. I ventured inside. I could hear a radio playing. A stand-up comedian was doing a monologue. The bar was far from ready to open. The counter was still nothing but a wooden frame. One wall had been knocked down, and the rubble hadn't been cleared. The sound of the radio came from the rear of the premises, so I continued on through. in a large room with a fireplace, a painter was at work, carefully painting the frame of a mirror.

"Sorry to bother you. I'm looking for Madeleine Barteau."

He switched off the radio and came down from his perch.

He had a blotchy face and very clear blue eyes. From the way he wrung out his brush, and how clean his hands were in the middle of all that mess, you could see he wasn't an amateur.

"Sorry?"

"I'm looking for Madeleine Barteau."

"Oh, the girl! It isn't her time, my friend, you'll have to wait a bit. What do you want with her?"

"I lent her some money. I can't seem to reach her."

That was how I presented it. A creditor showing up at a site was credible. I wasn't going to tell him my whole life story.

"Well, I hope you have stamina."

"Is it as bad as that?"

"You see this place? I'm starting on the finishing touches here while they're still taking the other side apart. It's all like that. Him, I saw once and then goodbye, I wonder if he's on the run. She's his puppet. She doesn't decide anything. She doesn't have the money. She talks to him on the phone for hours, but nothing ever happens. She acts like she's the boss, but if you want my opinion, he's stringing her along. The thing is, he must have tried to get a few local bigwigs to come in on this surefire deal of his, and when that didn't work, he made himself scarce, and she's going to end up in the shit. As far as getting paid is concerned, I'm not holding out much hope. The only reason I'm finishing the job is for my reputation, not for anything else. Do they owe you a lot?"

"Quite a bit. Around what time does she get here?"

"Sometimes she doesn't come at all!"

"I don't suppose you know where she lives?"

"Not far from here. In a hotel that rents out rooms. It's in a dead-end street at the end of Rue des Carterets. I had to go there and wake her once, because of a supplier who was kicking up a fuss."

"So she doesn't have an apartment?"

"No, that's his. He managed to get a loft, just to show off.

But it's over between them, he has other girls now. You should see his suit, his watch. Once he's had what he wants from them . . . "

I left the bar. The light blinded me. Rue des Carterets started at the corner. I just had to walk a few yards to get to it. It was a fairly narrow but very long street, which started in the rather classy pedestrian zone, and ended up in a noticeably more down-market neighborhood where some of the buildings were being demolished. The dead-end street was tiny, and the hotel the only one. The front was almost black, and an endless crack ran down it from top to bottom. It must have been collapsing on its foundations and, to stop it sinking any more, it was being held up on its right side by beams, like a crutch.

I stopped outside the front door. A sign indicated the prices, by the day or the month. Given the kind of place it was, they weren't cheap. I rang the doorbell and a very stout individual came and opened. He was wearing pants that were too short for him and he took up the whole width of the narrow corridor. A strange character. His face made him look like an enormous infant. He looked me up and down suspiciously, then moved away from the door to let me in. Once he was sure I didn't want to rob his till or deal drugs in his hotel, he had no objection to my going up. He even apologized for the fact that he couldn't warn Mademoiselle Barteau because the house phone was out of order. Personally, that was fine by me.

Madeleine was living on the top floor, in the attic, where the rates were cheapest. The fat man had told me the number of her room. It was the one that was missing. As I approached the door, she came out. She was in her nightdress, her hair was disheveled, and she was barefoot. She stood there for a few seconds in shock.

"I was just going to the toilet. Go in. I'll be right back."

I went in. The room was tiny, the ceiling blistered and

swollen. A single bed occupied one side of the room and, facing it, wedged in between the drainpipe and a narrow chest of drawers, was a table with an electric hotplate on it. I sat down on the bed. A small transom in the ceiling was slightly open, letting in a little fresh air as well as daylight. My eyes came to rest on my sister's bag, the one she took with her everywhere. It was filled to the brim, as if she was about to leave, or maybe had never even unpacked it. I saw a keyring hanging from one of the handles. I hadn't noticed it when she came to the house, but I knew that keyring. She'd always had it. When she was a little girl, it had adorned her school bag. It depicted a cartoon character who was always getting into trouble. I tried to remember his name. At that moment she came back from the toilet. She lifted her hand to her hair and pushed it back.

"Why didn't you warn me?"

"The time it would have taken me to get hold of you, I thought it was quicker to just come. I dropped by the bar. I saw the painter. He drew me a picture of the situation."

"Is that meant to be funny?"

"Unintentionally."

She must have felt like killing me at that moment. I could see it in her eyes. I'd landed in her real world. I was so close to her, it was indecent. She couldn't retreat, or run away. She grabbed hold of the chest of drawers. She decided to fight back, in spite of everything.

"If you're worried about your money—"

"I don't care about that."

"At least let me finish. Right now, Patrice is negotiating with a new partner. We underestimated the cost of the work, that's true, but—"

"Stop."

"He's coming back and then everything will get back to normal. Now's not the time to—"

"Stop, Madeleine!"

The impact of my voice in that little room hit her full in the chest.

"You're just like Ma. Don't you realize? You lie to save face and you end up believing in what you say. You choose men who beat you or humiliate you, just like her. But that's your business. It's your life. I'm not here to pass judgment. I came because of Léonard. Because he has nothing to do with any of this."

"I've always protected Léonard. You know, his father—"

"You didn't leave him, he left you. You'd still be with him, otherwise. And your son would be locked up. Like now!"

"That's a horrible thing to say. He needs treatment, that's all."

"He isn't a schizophrenic."

"So you're a psychiatrist now?"

"He has Asperger's syndrome. It isn't a disease. It's a different way of looking at things. He absolutely mustn't be isolated, that's the worst solution of all. He needs two things: to be recognized as someone who's different, which you haven't done, and then to be accepted as he is, which your men haven't done, and when that happens the only solution you can find is to push him away."

This time, she was stunned. I saw that from the way her hands lost their grip on the chest of drawers and she almost collapsed, like a boxer on the ropes.

"He's the one who wanted to go there. The psychiatrist explained it was what he was asking for with his fits of temper."

"And why do you think that is? To protect himself from you, and from me, too, because I let him leave."

Madeleine adjusted her dressing gown, and we stood there in silence, brother and sister, face-to-face, in that tiny room. The fight was over. The blows had hit home, it was finished. There was nothing more to defend, nothing to hide. She seemed to relax. Even her voice changed, becoming more human.

"What do you want to do?"

"Get him out of there."

"You won't be able to."

"Give me a proxy. I'll do the rest."

"He's never been like this before. He stopped playing chess. He broke his chess set."

"Give me that proxy."

35

I looked for a store that sold board games. Back in the vicinity of the cathedral, I found one easily. The man behind the counter looked like Don Quixote. He was also the owner, and as soon as I went in, he started talking to me about posterity, it was his obsession. He'd never had children, and it hurt him that when he died there was no son to take over the shop. I listened to him politely, but in the end had to tell him that I was in a hurry. I could see how disappointed he was that he couldn't confide in me anymore. He laid out several different kinds of chess set on his counter. I didn't hesitate. A good quality set in a small black box struck me as the right choice.

The Marcel Blanchet Medical and Psychiatric Center was situated in the north of the town, in a neighborhood that also housed the pound and an incinerator. The uses an area of land is put to sometimes says a lot about a society. The building was a former school that had been closed down after a fire because it did not conform to safety standards. For mental patients, the risk must have been more acceptable. I presented my credentials at the entrance. I showed them the proxy my sister had signed and my identity card, and went to the waiting room, as I'd been told to do. It was lunch hour for the patients, and they were all in the canteen. I wouldn't be able to see my nephew until after lunch. When I finally found a chair that wasn't rickety, which took a while, I opened the exercise book that Léonard had left in his room when he left. I needed to revise a little. I plunged back into his world, the diagonals, the indirect attacks, the reverse defenses, everything that made up the art of chess, which he'd mastered to the point of making it accessible. I forgot where I was, and what might be disturbing about it, to the extent that when the nurse came to fetch me I gave a start.

I followed her down corridors that were distinctly maze-like. It struck me that she was flustered by what I was doing, and that in informing me of Léonard's mental condition, which she described as worrying, she was implying that taking him out of the clinic wasn't the right decision. I didn't answer her. She stopped abruptly, as if her mind had wandered on the way and she'd forgotten the reason she was escorting me. She unlocked a door and let me in. Léonard was there, with his back to me, sitting on a bench.

I sat down next to him, but not too close, and at first I didn't speak. It reminded me of the early days of our relationship. But it wasn't a problem, I'd gotten to him. I waited a while longer, until I thought that now was the moment. I took the chess set out of my bag and put it down between the two of us. Of course, he didn't look at it. But he knew perfectly well what it was.

"You see. I came to keep my promise."

He didn't reply immediately. He was staring at the horrible plate-glass window, covered in dust, which looked out on a children's playground that had turned into a minefield.

"I only play with good players. Otherwise I get bored."

"Aren't I a good player?"

"No."

"How do you know, if we don't play?"

"It takes years to learn."

"Sometimes you can learn faster with a good teacher."

"Do you have a teacher?"

"I have his exercise book. He gave it to me."

"I think he forgot it."

"Maybe. Maybe not."

Léonard was still staring straight ahead. His face was impassive, but now that I knew him better, I could see signs that had escaped me at first. His lashes were fluttering. He must be faced with a choice, a difficulty to resolve.

I opened the box and started laying out the pieces. They were of precious wood, a real work of craftsmanship. The man without children hadn't cheated me when he sold me that model. Léonard changed his position, slowly, to face the chessboard. Then he waited for me to begin the game. In six moves, I was checkmated.

"You see, I made mincemeat of you."

"That doesn't mean I'm a bad player. It's just that you're very good. I'd like to play another game."

"You'll lose again."

"I know."

"Isn't it humiliating?"

"No. I'm learning a lot."

He looked up at me. I hadn't expected him to do that so soon. I let him start this time, and of course he won. But I didn't care.

36

I called Catherine as I was filling up with gas at a service station. I told her I was bringing Léonard back. My mother had woken and had even taken a few steps in the corridor. According to Dr. Vandrecken, she was perfectly lucid. She wanted to have a good meal and had given instructions about it to Catherine, calling her her "daughter- in-law." A leg of lamb was waiting for us, with sautéed potatoes: the favorite dish of Gabrielle Barteau, née Lemoine. As for us, our mission was to bring back some cakes, including a real mille-feuille for my mother.

On the way, Léonard asked me for news of the team. I told him about the defeat by Valenciennes. I didn't insist on Favelic's performance. Rather, we talked about tactics, the danger of defending too deep and in too large numbers, which meant cutting the team in two and isolating the strikers.

"Fear makes people lose," Léonard said.

I agreed. He was concerned to know when the championship was starting and, when he discovered there was only a week to go, I could sense he was weighing up his chances of getting his place back. But I didn't want to talk about that, I didn't want to build castles in the air, it depended on so many things. I thought about my sister in her hotel room, with the hot plate on the table and the toilet on the landing. I remembered the name of the character on her keyring. It was Calimero. The black chicken that wore an eggshell instead of a hat and was always getting into trouble.

We scoured all the pastry shops in Sedan searching for a decent mille-feuille. We found lots of imitations, but none really convinced us, until we got lost in the maze of streets and came across a simple bakery that had only two kinds of cakes, rum babas and mille-feuilles. Léonard asked to taste the custard, in that slightly irritating voice of his, and I thought we were going to be thrown out, but against all expectation, the baker's wife took us into the backroom where her husband made the cakes, and this scary-looking man who must have been about seven feet tall took a bowl filled with custard from a cold cabinet. Obviously, it was the right kind, and we walked off with what was left in the window.

The house had never smelled like that before. The smell of grilled meat, potatoes simmering, a family Sunday. Catherine Vandrecken really was a surprising person. Now she was a housewife with a cloth over her shoulder, cutting fresh garlic into thin slices.

"You should buy some good knives."

"It smells amazing."

"I hope so."

Léonard sat down on the edge of the bed and placed his hand on his grandmother's. She opened her eyes, as if she'd been waiting for that signal. What happened at that moment seemed to me to defy understanding. Better than morphine, better than anything, Léonard's presence gave my mother sufficient strength to get up. She wanted to go into the garden. She wanted to eat outside, to take advantage of the sun. I began by telling her she had to be sensible, but she forced me to go out and see what the weather was like, and I had to admit it was one of those fall days that are like spring.

I didn't have to negotiate with Catherine, who'd heard my mother's request from a distance and was already holding one side of the kitchen table. I took the other, and we put it out on the terrace behind the house. Then Léonard laid it. It was the middle of the afternoon, but nobody bothered about that. We were hungry.

We sat down at the table, Léonard next to his grand-mother, Catherine and I facing each other. I cut the leg of lamb, and we ate it without speaking. My mother wanted to taste the wine. A Côte-Rôtie the same age as Léonard. She spilled a little on her blouse and laughed like a little girl. The sun was on her back. She was feeling fine. She congratulated Catherine on the food, and told me I was lucky. I tried to tell her we weren't married, but it was no use. Suddenly, her expression changed and she asked why Madeleine wasn't there. I told her she had a new job, which was very time-con-suming, but she would come as soon as she could. My mother appeared to think this over, then changed the subject and told Léonard how, at the age of five, he had regularly beat her at checkers. He pretended not to remember. I cleared the table with Catherine, and we did the dishes together. I washed, she wiped.

"Thank you," I said.

"That shirt really suits you."

I'd grabbed that white shirt from my closet just before the meal. I'd never worn it before and it still had the fold marks. We got the dessert plates ready, and put the cakes on a dish. A choice of mille-feuille or rum baba.

When we went back out on the terrace, my mother was standing up. It struck me as unreal, but it was true. Léonard was next to her. She was gazing out at that little garden as if it was the Pacific Ocean.

"I'd like to walk with you a little," she said to me. She could sense my reluctance, but clutched my arm. "To the bottom of the garden, and no further. Please."

We walked across the carpet of dead leaves that had fallen from the surrounding trees. We reached the end of the lawn, almost easily. My mother weighed nothing, but her steps were sure. She wanted to carry on, along the fence, as far as a cherry tree under which there was a worm-eaten wooden bench with rusty legs that was currently in the sun. She sat down, without giving me any choice. From there, she could see the yard and hear Catherine and Léonard teasing each other as they put the dessert plates on the table.

"When I was little," my mother said, "I had a doll house and a collection of rag dolls. I used to play with them. I called them the Rapon family. I loved that house. But when we moved, the house broke and I never found the dolls. I looked for them for years . . . I wanted . . . a family, you know. I hadn't been brought up by my parents. I was ready to do anything to keep that family . . . "

"We don't need to talk about that."

"But I want to talk about it."

Her mouth was trembling and her fists were clenched. I sensed that I mustn't stop her.

"I could see your father was losing his mind. But I thought I could keep my house,

that it would work out. I sent Madeleine away. That was why she was a boarder. You, I thought . . . you were so strong, even when you were small. I thought, he'll leave anyway, he doesn't need anybody . . . "

"Did you really think that?"

"Yes."

The sun disappeared. All at once, it started to feel cooler under the bare tree.

"We have to go back to the table, Ma."

"Wait a while longer. I have one regret. I never held you in my arms, and now it's too late."

We were on that bench, the two of us. I put my arms around her.

"You're doing it for me."

"Yes. It's my turn."

We stayed like that, motionless, under the cherry tree, then a shiver went through her.

"Does it hurt?"

"No."

"Come and eat your mille-feuille."

There was still a ray of sunshine lighting the terrace. My mother cut her cake. She was an expert on mille-feuilles. She tipped it onto its side so that the custard didn't all come out when the knife went through.

"It's the real thing," she said.

I stood up to make coffee. I put in the filter and filled the beaker with water. I heard a muffled cry and rushed out. My mother had fallen off her chair without warning, and Catherine was trying to lift her, but her body was limp and her eyes glazed over. I carried her to her bed, while Catherine called her friend, Dr. Mérieux. Barely a quarter of an hour later, he was there. He spent quite a while in the bedroom, then came out to give us his diagnosis. She wouldn't regain consciousness. It was the end.

"How long?"

"A few hours, maybe tonight."

"Is she in pain?"

"No. Not anymore."

I had mislaid my phone. When I found it again, I discovered that my sister had left a message. She started to say something, then gave up, left a long silence, and finally explained that the number displayed was hers, that she'd bought a cell phone at last. I called her back immediately and got her mailbox. I tried to be clear and concise. Our mother was going to die that night. She'd fallen into a coma so suddenly that I hadn't been able to tell her earlier.

Léonard had taken refuge in his room, and Catherine had joined him there. He'd put his head on her chest. She was talking to him softly.

I went back to my mother. From time to time, her breathing got out of control, then became regular again. I saw that her ring had almost slipped off her finger, and I adjusted it. My father had given it to her on their fifteenth anniversary, accompanying this gift with a whole performance. He'd had the car washed. He took my mother to a posh restaurant, while we stayed at home, left to our own devices. But it was only years later I heard the real story, when I ran into the jeweler who'd sold him that ring. He was retired now, and he recognized me from all the times he'd shooed me away from the doorway of his shop, where I'd stop to eat ice cream I'd bought from the bakery opposite. At the time, he'd accused me of scaring away his customers, but now he didn't care about any of that. I'd become a valuable witness of the old days when he'd still been active, and he confessed, as he would to a friend, that the famous ring was a fake. And he added that in spite of its modest cost—modest for such an impressive-looking ring—my father had asked if he could pay him in three installments, and that he'd never received the final installment.

Catherine came into the room and walked up to me. When she saw my hand lying on my mother's, she left us alone again. I'd listened to Gabrielle under the bare cherry tree, and now I was answering her, although nobody could hear my words.

I closed the door of the room on the way out and crossed the corridor. Léonard had fallen asleep. I went to the kitchen. I needed wine. The back door was open. I took my glass out with me. Catherine was sitting looking out at the night. On the table, the cakes were still there, my mother's mille-feuille only just started.

"Well?"

"She seems peaceful. And Léonard?"

"He wanted to know what becomes of bodies after death. What happens to them in cemeteries, if the coffin rots in the ground, if it gets moved, that kind of thing."

"I think he also wanted your warmth."

I put my legs up on a chair and knocked back my drink in one go. I felt the effect of the liquid throughout my body. An owl could be heard in the distance. On the other side of the fence, there was a row of houses, but after that, open countryside. I'd never realized that before.

"You're starting to get a taste for wine."

"Yes."

"You should try the rum baba. Do you think your sister will come?"

"That's up to her. I didn't go to my father's funeral, you know. I forgot all about it. What about you?"

"Me?"

"Are your parents still alive?"

"No."

"Is there a connection with the terrified little girl?"

"Of course. My mother always went for walks on the banks of the Seine with my little sister Lucie. We lived in the sixteenth arrondissement in Paris, in a nice apartment, a bourgeois apartment, you could call it. My father was a well-known architect, my mother didn't work but didn't seem to mind. My father didn't know what to do to spoil her. Not a day went by that he didn't buy her a gift. She was always well turned out, always looked wonderful. She threw herself in the Seine, holding my little sister's hand. Lucie's body was found three days later, in a lock, my mother's never was. Had she been planning it for a long time? Or did she act on impulse? Nobody knows. There were no clues. No painful family history, no thwarted ambition. Genetics maybe? My maternal grandfather killed himself with his hunting rifle. My father was someone who believed in logic. He couldn't bear not knowing the reason for his wife's suicide. His body gave way, he had leukemia, in six months he was gone. I'd always thought he was indestructible. He'd never had a cold. I clung to my studies, my books, to knowledge, as if was a life raft."

"In order to understand."

"Yes, or at least to try. You know, for years, an image haunted me. My little sister seeing herself dragged into the water . . . "

"They drown themselves. And they try to take us with them."

"Who?"

"Our parents."

"When we met, in the hospital . . . I dreamed about you the following night. You were on the riverbank. You took Lucie in your arms. She was saved."

"It was just a dream."

"It's possible sometimes, isn't it?"

"We have to save ourselves first."

"Do you think I'm shameless?"

"No, I wish I had your courage."

"Do I still scare you?"

"Less than before."

38

Madeleine arrived late. She'd taken the last train from Rheims, and had had to change at Charleville. In Sedan, she'd walked before finding a taxi. Her hair was a mess, and she wasn't wearing foundation this time, just her real face. She went and kissed Léonard and pulled up his blanket, then went into our mother's room. I left them both to get on with it. She must have things to say to her, too. By the time I returned, Catherine had put on her coat.

"Are you leaving?"

"I have to go to my office."

"At this hour?"

"I dropped everything to come here. I have to sort things out for tomorrow."

She came toward me. I thought she was going to kiss me, but she adjusted my shirt collar.

"And besides, if we become too close, you won't like it. I prefer to be the one to walk away. I have my pride, you know.

I went back to the yard to finish clearing up. The temperature had fallen noticeably and the oilcloth glistened with damp and cold. I put the cakes in the fridge. I suddenly thought of the leak. I opened the closet under the sink. The bucket was almost full. I grabbed it to empty it. Just then, my sister came out of the bedroom.

"What are you doing with that bucket?"

"I have a leak and I can't turn off the water at the meter. It starts vibrating and making an incredible racket."

"Where's your boiler?"

"In the basement."

"How do you get there?"

"The door next to the front door."

"You take my place with Ma, I'll have a look."

She was already on the stairs. I went back to my mother. I realized that her wig had slipped slightly to the side of her head. I tried to adjust it, but my hand slipped, and I felt it come away completely. I found myself with that clump of synthetic hair in my hands, and my mother's head, bare, on the pillow. Going with a friend to maternity, a few years earlier, I'd been struck by how much like old people newborn babies look in the first hours after delivery. This was exactly the opposite: an old person with the head of a baby. I adjusted the wig as best I could. I didn't touch anything else. From the depths of the house, strange noises reached me, which turned into a disturbing whistle, then all at once silence returned. Soon afterwards, my sister signaled to me to join her in the kitchen. Her hands were black and she was rubbing them vigorously with a brush. I saw that the bucket was next to her. I made to put it back in its place.

"You don't need it anymore."

"Did you cut off the water?"

"Better still, I repaired the leak. These miracle glues are a scam. It's better to simply change the part. Didn't you see you had a whole stock of them in the basement, elbows, straight pipes, clamps?"

"No. I never go down there."

"And as for the vibrations, I fixed that too. Basically, the faucet that should have been closed was open, and the one that should have been open was closed."

She talked about plumbing with amazing naturalness, rather the way Léonard talked about chess.

"Oh, and by the way, your basement door is terrible. It needs planing."

"I hate DIY."

"Because of Dad?"

"It's nothing to do with Dad."

"Oh, yes? I love it. Don't you remember I used to repair your toy trucks? You'd bring them to me and I had to fix them come what may. You used to call me Reparator."

"I don't remember."

"Really?"

"Really."

"When I was fourteen, I wanted to get a qualification as a car mechanic. I made inquiries, they took girls, I loved body-work."

"So why secretarial school?

"To please Ma. She wanted me to become a private secretary and marry my boss. She was convinced that was my future."

"It didn't quite work out that way."

"No. Not quite."

She wiped her hands. She was bathed in sweat, but she was twice as strong as when she'd arrived.

"Why don't you stay?"

"What?"

"Nothing works in this house. You could fix it up. You'd be Reparator. It'd give you time to turn yourself around. To think about what you really want to do."

"I don't want to leach off you."

"Who said anything about that? You'll be doing a job and I'll pay you. You know, a coach earns quite a bit, and I never spend it on anything."

"Certainly not on clothes."

"What do you mean?"

"Nothing. It's kind of you but I have to get back to Rheims, I have to see this thing through."

"See what through? Getting screwed over, like Ma?"

174 · ALAIN GILLOT

Tears suddenly rose to her eyes. Something in her wanted to believe in another possible life, but she couldn't.

"Don't go thinking it's for you. It's an offer that suits me. If I don't have Léonard in my team, we'll be wiped out in the championship, but without his mother, it won't work for long. He's a genius, but he's still a kid."

"Is he as good as that?"

"You have no idea."

"So you actually have an ulterior motive."

"Of course."

"You still have a heart of stone."

"Yes."

"I was afraid you'd changed."

It was at that moment that Léonard appeared. We hadn't heard him coming. He was like a little ghost. His face was impassive, his voice calm. He'd gone to see his grandmother when he woke up.

"I think she's stopped breathing," he said.

39

Three days later we buried Gabrielle Barteau, née Lemoine, in the cemetery in Saint-Quentin, where she'd bought a plot on my father's death. Only my sister and I were there to see the coffin lowered into the hole next to André Abel Barteau. After the slab was closed, Madeleine went to buy a geranium to decorate it a little, and we ate sandwiches, sitting on the grave. I remembered the advice my mother had given her to become a private secretary and marry her boss. I couldn't believe she could have said that.

"Basically, she was stupid," my sister said.

She raised her hand to her mouth as soon as she'd uttered these sacrilegious words, as if a thunderbolt from heaven would come down and strike us. But there wasn't a cloud in the sky, it was so sunny you felt like taking your jacket off, and the punishment never came.

Then I left for Rheims to collect Madeleine's things from the hotel on Rue des Carterets. We agreed that I'd go alone, in case Patrice was around and turned violent. But when I passed the bar, just to take a look, I saw that the place was sealed up.

The match with Châteauroux was fast approaching. Léonard found his way to the locker room and I could see from the way his teammates looked at him how relieved they were that he was back. Their dear Martian. During the training session that followed, I was also able to verify the thing that people say about talent, that it spreads. By being absent, Léonard had made the boys think about that extra bit of spirit that was missing from their game, and his return drove them to give more of themselves. Cosmin had always been brilliant, but up until now, he'd never gone out of his comfort zone. He'd make space for himself, monopolize the ball, but when it came down to it he seldom played a key role. I'd abandoned hope, but now, suddenly, I had the feeling his game might develop in a more collective direction. Even Rouverand, who only ever judged a match by the number of opportunities it gave him to score, turned at moments into a center forward worthy of the name. He didn't just wait for a ball to come into the penalty area, but showed that he was capable of participating in a genuine offensive, one put together by the whole team. All the same, Châteauroux, whom we were due to meet for that inaugural match, was rather a high mountain to climb. Their premier team was in Division 2, with a good chance of promotion to Division 1, and their training center was considered a breeding ground for some of the best talents in the whole of France.

The great day arrived. The club had given us the Auguste Deylaud stadium, where the field was as smooth as a billiard table. We arrived by minibus and invaded the locker room, which struck us as strangely large in relation to our much reduced group. I'd decided that Cosmin would be captain. It was a gamble, I knew. He could either grow even more given that responsibility, or give in to his demons, precisely because he'd been singled out from his teammates. He and I did a rapid reconnaissance of the ground to see how supple it was and to choose the type of cleat appropriate to it. I looked up at the sky. Heavy clouds were coming in from the east.

There were lots of spectators in the stands and at the edge of the field. The management of the club had come to see what the future might look like, and most of the parents were there. In less than two hours, all these people would either be carrying me in triumph or demanding my head on a platter.

Catherine Vandrecken arrived with my sister. She was wear-

ing a raincoat and a cap that gave her a mischievous air. I kept
my distance and saw Meunier introduce himself. He didn't
waste any time, I thought. As she spoke to him, Catherine met
my eyes and gave me a little sign. I responded with a nod and
went into the corridor leading to the locker room. I opted for
a very short pep talk. The boys were sufficiently afraid of their
opponents to be focused. I insisted on one point, not to play
too deep, not to be too defensive, as we had against
Valenciennes, but to keep pressing forward, and I also spoke
about the weather, which might play a crucial role. I was convinced that the rain would start falling very soon, and I encour-
aged my players to go all out for the first fifteen minutes, on
dry ground, in order to be able to play for time later if the playing conditions became difficult.

The boys came out of the locker room making a noise with
their cleats. Léonard was the last out. I held him back by his
shirt. It was his first official match. I insisted on the need to
keep his self-control, whatever happened, but I made it clear
that my warning wasn't connected with his Asperger's, it was
just that anyone playing in a tournament for the first time
might not necessarily realize the consequences of a rude ges-
ture or one word too many to the referee.

The players walked onto the pitch. The Châteauroux players were on average four inches taller than mine, with muscles
to match. The captains exchanged pennants and the two teams
got into position. I passed Madeleine on my way to the touchline. She'd had her hair cut and looked her natural color again.

"She's beautiful, isn't she?"

"Who are you talking about?"

"You know perfectly well. Catherine. Are you still friends?"

"More than ever."

The match started dramatically. Immediately on kick-off,
Bensaid passed to Cosmin, who looked for Rouverand and
sent the ball flying through the air over the opposing team's

wall of defenders. There was a one-in-ten chance of it working, but the ball ended up just in front of Kevin, who didn't think twice and sent it zooming straight down the middle, while the Châteauroux goalkeeper was scratching himself, and the poor boy saw the ball brush past his shoulder without reacting. 1–0 to us. A perfect shot. Any other team apart from our opponents would probably have been knocked senseless after a start like that, but in this case it was as if a deadly machine had been set in motion. The power and organization of Châteauroux came into their own, with an onslaught on Léonard's goal. I thought at that point, and so did everyone on the edge of the field, that our advantage would collapse in an instant. The disparity between our opponents and us, in terms of athletic potential, as well as organization on the field, was too obvious. Except that wasn't exactly what happened. Châteauroux kept taking chances, but nothing worked. Sometimes the ball grazed the bar, or went just over the head of an unmarked striker but didn't go into the net. And when finally the goal seemed open, and an equalizer looked inevitable, it was Léonard who intervened, thanks to one of his brilliant anticipatory moves, which were becoming his trademark.

It had started raining, and you could feel the tension on the field. The delayed goal not only hadn't thrown Châteauroux, it had given them extra strength. At the same time, the fact that they hadn't equalized quickly, or even after persistent effort, increased their frustration. A first deadly tackle on Mutu set the tone for a match that had tipped over into excessive aggression. Châteauroux couldn't lose, but their patience was exhausted, their pride hurt. As they kept pushing forward, the atmosphere became heavier. They were awarded a corner kick. As the ball came down, Léonard was ideally placed, and was getting ready to grab it when a foot hit his face with unprecedented violence. It came from Châteauroux's center forward, a blond guy who looked like a pitbull, and who'd launched himself into a high-risk attempt to get the ball back, with the evident desire to hurt the player who'd been resisting them for far too long. Léonard collapsed, although without letting go of the ball. I rushed forward. I didn't think for a second. Had the referee blown the whistle? I didn't give a damn. I ran as if in slow motion toward my nephew, and entered the penalty area. A fight had started between the center forward and Marfaing. Other players joined in, it was complete chaos. I pushed my way through to reach Léonard. He was trying to get up, but nobody was paying any attention to him, everybody was focused on the fight. There he was, on his knees, swaying a little, but his face was still totally calm, even though it was covered in blood. I tried to get to him, but at that moment I was grabbed firmly by the arm. I broke free angrily to confront whoever was trying to stop me coming to my nephew's aid and screamed my anger in his face, my fear, too, because of the assault he'd just been subjected to. All the insults I knew came out of my mouth.

The referee faced me. It was he who'd grabbed my arm, he who was now weighing up how dangerous I was, expressive vocabulary. He didn't hesitate for long. He stepped back, took a red card from his pocket, and pointed to the locker rooms, while his assistants tried to hold me back. I turned to Léonard. He was still in the same place, as if frozen. He'd clearly taken to heart my advice before the match to never lose control. I was thrown off the field and led back to the locker rooms. Sitting on a bench, I could hear the noise of the stadium, the protests, the whistles, which lasted several more minutes before the match apparently resumed. I kicked the door and hurt myself. I cried out, alone in those cold locker rooms. I walked up and down like a caged animal, then finally sat down again on the bench. Catherine came in. That was all I needed.

"Well?" I asked.

"The match has started again."

"And Léonard?"

"He's in his place. It was just the arch of the eyebrow. It looks worse than it is."

"Did you see that assault! It's unacceptable. And that stupid referee sending me off. What about the other guy, the center forward, did he send him off, too?"

"No."

"It's a scandal!"

"Vincent, there's no point losing your temper."

"How can I not lose my temper over something so unfair! He was almost decapitated by that killer!"

"You love that kid."

"What?"

"You love him."

"It's not about that! You don't understand anything! He was in the penalty area!"

"And?"

"You can't do that in the penalty area! It's taboo!"

"Taboo, eh? Interesting."

"Are you making fun of me?"

"I'd never dare."

"Oh, yes, I see what you're up to, Madam Psychiatrist, but I'm not playing with words, I'm talking about the rules of soccer, the ethics of the referee's profession! Everything falls to pieces if you flout those principles! And they were being flouted, don't you see?"

"You have a scratch."

"What?

At that moment Catherine came up to me. I recoiled slightly.

"I'm not going to hurt you. Show me that."

"It's nothing, it was when they dragged me off the field, I struggled and—"

"They scored a second goal, you know. The one called Cosmin."

"What? A second goal? Couldn't you have told me that earlier?"

"Yes, if you'd given me time. We'll have to disinfect it anyway. Are you up to date with your vaccinations? I'm sure you aren't."

"It's nothing, I tell you!

She was very close to me. Her cap was pushed back a little. She took me by surprise and kissed me.

"What did you just do?"

"I kissed you."

"You don't have any right to do that."

"Are there rules for that too?"

"Of course! There are rules for everything."

L éonard has appointed himself supervisor of the garden. Since early afternoon, he's been carefully raking the dead leaves, taking care to preserve the most beautiful ones in a large book. I suspect him of wanting to feel what neurotypical children feel, the ones who are called normal, by indulging in this kind of simple activity. He's been fascinated for a while with particles, particularly the Higgs boson. He asked me to buy him everything serious I could find about on the birth of the universe, and I saw that he was devoting a brand-new exercise book to this question. It seems to me that his way of playing is influenced by this growing interest in the cosmos. He's increasingly comfortable with high-flying balls and unpredictable trajectories.

My sister is plastering the walls of her son's room. From a distance, I can hear her trowel scraping the porous surface with great precision and regularity. It's incredible how quickly she works once she's decided on an area that needs attention. Yesterday, she removed that horrible wallpaper. Last week, she rewired the house.

Tomorrow, she plans to tackle her own room by knocking down the wall facing the garden and putting in a picture window. Of course this outburst of DIY isn't without its disadvantages. It's quite difficult, at times, to find anything in the place where it was the day before. At first that bothered me enormously, but I'm gradually adapting. It's Catherine Vandrecken's pet theory about boxes that's gaining ground in my narrow sportsman's brain. Having few boxes, always knowing where they are, allows man to adapt rapidly to his environment, but, being terribly reductive, this simplicity also limits him. To agree to increase the number of boxes, to question their relevance, to invent new ones when the need arises: that takes more time, for sure, but gives you a multitude of extra possibilities. And maybe quite simply helps you to feel freer.

I've sat down on the bench under the cherry tree. I come here regularly now, to talk with my mother. With my father, too, even though I didn't know him so well. I'm more and more convinced that on the day of his accident, he deliberately swerved into the ditch. Rather the way Catherine's mother threw herself in the Seine. Except that we weren't in the car. I don't resent André and Gabrielle anymore. Who would ever have thought that possible? Life is long, we probably don't realize how long. My parents didn't have many boxes. They adapted too quickly. They were so afraid of being rejected that they must have pretended to know before they started to learn. It's thanks to Léonard that I've understood some of these complex things. That particle that crossed my sky.

Madeleine has come out of the house. She walks toward me. She's wearing the sweater she's dedicated to her art. It's streaked with different colored paint stains, and has burns from the soldering iron and cuts from the saw. Her face is spattered with bits of plaster, her hands reddened from holding the tools, several fingers covered with bandages. She smiles, she's half dead with exhaustion, but she's happy.

"Aren't you answering your phone?"

"I don't know where it is. Don't ask me why."

"Don't go blaming the work. Catherine called me in the end, because she couldn't reach you. She'll be here, but not until seven-thirty. An emergency at the hospital."

"What do you mean she'll be here? We see each other on Tuesdays."

"You know, I wonder if you haven't gone straight from wisdom to senility. Today is Tuesday."

I rush into the bathroom. I still have half an hour, I can thank the hospital for that. Madeleine drops everything to iron a shirt for me, and Léonard starts searching for the leather moccasins I've just paid a fortune for, to replace my everlasting sneakers. In the end he has to admit defeat. They might be in a box my sister took down to the basement when she emptied my room to build a bookcase, but since the basement door is obstructed by a mountain of wood being stored there temporarily, he prefers to throw in the towel.

Catherine rings the doorbell. She's come straight from her office. Her hair is loose and she has rings under her eyes, which is how I like her best, the ultimate expression of her sensuality.

"Sorry I'm late."

"I'll forgive you this time."

She kisses me, then holds me close and looks me in the eyes. "What's that ironic look?" she asks.

"It isn't for you, it's for me."

"We'll be just in time for the movie."

"We can eat beforehand and go to the last show. Or else not go at all."

"Do you mind?"

"Not a bit."

"There's a weird smell here."

"Madeleine's started on the plaster in Léonard's room."

"Oh."

We leave without disturbing them. They're both in their own worlds. From the sidewalk, we can see life inside the house. Madeleine on her stool, Léonard engrossed in a book.

"The house looks bigger, doesn't it?"

"That's because it's lived in."

We leave the car and walk. Catherine sees that I've kept my awful sneakers and calls me a sportsman, to which I respond by calling her an intellectual. Sometimes, we like to play with the old boxes. In the meantime, I'm holding her arm.

It's already too late for the movies, and walking as slowly as we are, and being some distance from the center of town, there isn't much chance we'll find a restaurant still serving dinner in Sedan on a Tuesday evening. It doesn't really matter. We can just as easily have a drink sitting on a banquette in the station brasserie. All we want is to sit side by side and talk, smoke, drink, start talking again, then kiss like idiots. And when we're really hungry, we can always go back to the house and cook ham and eggs. And see my sister wander into the kitchen with her tub of plaster, and hear Léonard, having just emerged from his reading, explain the birth of the universe, his hands conducting an invisible orchestra: this family that has somehow formed, the one I spent so long looking for.

ABOUT THE AUTHOR

Alain Gillot is an admired journalist, a screenwriter, and a comic book author. *The Penalty Area* is his debut novel.